ENGAGEMENT WITH DEATH

Engagement with Death

A Patrick Dawlish Mystery

John Creasey *writing as* Gordon Ashe

OPEN ROAD

INTEGRATED MEDIA
NEW YORK

Copyright © 1948 by John Creasey

ISBN: 978-1-5040-9817-5

This edition published in 2025 by Open Road Integrated Media, Inc.
180 Maiden Lane
New York, NY 10038
www.openroadmedia.com

ENGAGEMENT WITH DEATH

CHAPTER ONE

REQUEST FROM AN ABSENT WIFE

'Do try to find out whether it is really true that Pop Fairweather intends to marry Georgette Lee.' Felicity wrote. 'I'm fond of the old boy and I'd hate to think of him making a fool of himself.'

'Paris is wonderful! It's like a breath of the old days . . .'

Patrick Dawlish read the rest of his wife's letter while a pair of kippers grew cold on his plate. Both letter and kippers finished at last, he was drinking his third cup of coffee when a remarkably tall, good-looking old man strode across the room, preceded by an obsequious steward and seated himself at a table in a window recess. Such tables at the Carilon Club were reserved for resident members only—and for some years 'Pop' Fairweather had been regarded as the Club's grand old man.

Dawlish read again that part of the letter which referred to Pop.

The *affaire* between Pop and Georgette Lee was common gossip in the West End, but to Dawlish it was news. Such chatter seldom permeated to his Surrey home, Haslemere not being concerned with London society gossip.

He gathered up the rest of his post, and walked towards the

door. This was his second morning in London since his wife had gone on a shopping spree to Paris. On the previous morning, he had seen Fairweather in a window seat in the smoking-room. Dawlish went now, to the same spot.

Several members looked at him over the tops of their papers. Two stewards hovered near, showing signs of dismay. Men entering the room glanced in surprise at seeing this very large, fair-haired man sitting in that sacrosanct window seat.

The chief steward approached him, hesitated, and then moved forward with an air of determination.

'Good morning, Major Dawlish.'

'Good morning,' said Dawlish.

The steward coughed.

'I wonder if you will mind me telling you—' He broke off in confusion, disconcerted by the steady gaze from Dawlish's cornflower blue eyes.

'Tell me exactly what you like,' invited Dawlish.

'Thank you, sir. It's just—well—that Mr. Fairweather usually sits here, sir!'

'Does he?' commented Dawlish.

'Every morning for the last three years he's sat here, sir, to be exact.'

At that moment Fairweather entered the smoking-room.

Whether or not he guessed that the chief steward was informing Dawlish of the enormity of his offence, it was impossible to say. The chief steward greeted him warmly and touched another chair.

'Shall I move this one round, sir?'

'If Major Dawlish would be so kind as to make room, yes,' said Fairweather.

'I'll be delighted,' said Dawlish, rising and pulling a second chair into position.

Both men settled themselves, rustling their papers.

There was no doubt that Pop's chair was awkwardly placed. Two members passed so close to him that he had to tuck in his legs, and a moment later a man coming from the other direction brushed against his *Times* with muttered apologies.

There were other interruptions during the next five minutes, and at last Fairweather looked at Dawlish, with something like a reproach in his eyes.

'Mr. Dawlish,' he began in a low-pitched voice. 'You may not be aware that you're occupying the chair I usually occupy, and—'

Dawlish leapt up.

'Am I really? I *am* sorry.' He waved at the now vacant chair with a charming smile. 'Do take it,' he invited.

'Thank you,' Fairweather said with a touch of sarcasm, as he rose and resettled himself. 'You're not often here, are you?'

'I live most of the year in the country,' said Dawlish. 'My wife is shopping in Paris at the moment, and so I'm a grass widower.'

'Wanted a change, I suppose,' remarked Fairweather. 'Typical of the age. Not that I don't think a change is good sometimes—a complete readjustment of one's life,' he continued. 'It's a bad thing to get set in one's ways.'

'I couldn't agree more,' said Dawlish.

'Of course, one expects criticism if one does anything unusual,' went on Fairweather, a little more heatedly than an abstract remark warranted. 'But if one closes one's ears to it, there's no need to be unduly concerned.'

'None whatever,' agreed Dawlish heartily.

Now that he had broken the ice with the old man, he was content enough to look through the newspapers. It might be several days before Pop reached the point of confiding in him; indeed, that point might never be reached. But anyhow, he could tell Felicity he'd made an effort.

Pop was something of an autocrat; and this was understandable in a millionaire bachelor with extensive business interests. Newspaper publicity and his trenchant comments on the folly of the young had combined to make him a public figure, regarded on the whole with affectionate amusement.

Georgette Lee, too, in her way was a public figure, renowned as an actress whose career was studded with short-lived romances. Perhaps the time had come, Dawlish thought, recalling his wife's letter, for her to see some measure of security.

There was no doubt that Pop was restless. At the end of twenty minutes, he had given up all pretence of reading, and was staring out of the window at the waving tree tops in the Mall. Now and again he shot a quick glance at Dawlish.

Ever mindful of Felicity's injunction Dawlish lowered his paper.

'There isn't much in the papers this morning,' he remarked casually.

'Very little—very little indeed,' Pop agreed. 'In my view, newspapers should deal in facts, not in expressions of biased and often illogical Opinions. Take *that* thing, for instance,' he went on with a disparaging stab at Dawlish's *Cry*. 'The news it contains could be put into half a column!' He snorted. 'The rest is a sensational distortion of facts.'

'I see your point of view,' said Dawlish pacifically.

'It's not a point of view, it's a statement of fact,' retorted Fairweather. 'I have frequently been the butt of such impertinence. Doubtless I shall be again.' He drew in his breath and stared fixedly at Dawlish. 'Dawlish, will you give me a frank answer to a somewhat unusual question?'

'Of course, if I can,' replied Dawlish.

'How do you regard marriage between an elderly man and a woman of, well, thirty shall we say?'

A picture of Georgette Lee appeared in Dawlish's mind; he thought thirty was deducting her of at least ten of her well-lived years.

'It depends on the two people concerned,' he said, evasively. 'Some men of seventy seem as young as others of forty—'

'That's precisely what I think,' said Fairweather. He drew his chair a little nearer to Dawlish. 'You will treat what I have to say in confidence, won't you?'

'Why, of course.'

'I am contemplating marriage,' announced Fairweather.

'Really! My dear sir, congratulations!'

'Very few people know—not even my closest friends believe I'm serious,' went on Fairweather, 'but having thought it over very carefully I've come to the conclusion that a quiet wedding is wiser than a fashionable one. Less publicity,' he added, clearing his throat. 'As a matter of fact I have even contemplated a secret wedding in a registry office.'

'May I ask the name of your fiancee?'

'I doubt whether you would know her personally,' said Fairweather, 'you're out of London so much.' He hesitated. 'I'm very interested to have your opinion,' he added, and turned back to his papers; this time he appeared to settle down.

Half an hour later, when Dawlish left the room, he received only a blank stare from Fairweather. He went downstairs to the porters' office and before leaving the club sent off a telegram to Felicity, reading: *I'm afraid you are right. Commiserations.*

During the next hour he thought a good deal about Fairweather's impending marriage. It was no concern of his and did not greatly matter to him; on the other hand, Felicity had been worried enough to write about it. He could not imagine the marriage being a success; Georgette had cast her spell over Pop, as she had over countless men.

Felicity was right, however, there was something grotesque in the very thought.

It was nearly twelve o'clock when he reached Piccadilly Circus and strolled towards the *Café Royal*, where he was to meet two friends. A newspaper van drew up with early 'evening' papers and dumped a packet of *Stars* at the stand near the end of Regent Street. Dawlish picked up a paper absently, and glanced down.

Georgette Lee smiled up at him from the front page.

By the side of the photograph ran the headline:

ACTRESS INJURED IN FLAT BURGLARY

CHAPTER TWO

POP FAIRWEATHER IN DISTRESS

Dawlish looked along Regent Street in the hope of seeing a disengaged taxi as Edward Beresford, one of the men whom he had come to meet, walked stiffly across the road. A taxi drew up and Dawlish climbed in, saying: 'Carilon Club, please.' As he slammed the door, he heard his name called.

'Pat!'

Dawlish leaned out of the window.

Beresford, a very large, ungainly man with an ugly face, looked at him indignantly.

'Sorry, Ted,' Dawlish said, 'but I may not be able to come. If I'm not back by half past twelve, you and Tim had better carry on without me.'

'But—'

'And if you've nothing better to do, make a few inquiries for me about Georgette Lee,' suggested Dawlish. 'All right, driver!'

'Georgette *who*?' boomed Beresford.

'Buy a *Star*,' advised Dawlish.

The cab moved off as Dawlish opened his own paper and began to read an account of the burglary.

Georgette had been found unconscious in her Mayfair flat by her daily maid at seven o'clock that morning. The actress was suffering from head injuries but her condition gave 'no cause for anxiety'. Her bedroom had been ransacked, her jewels and some loose money were missing.

The rest of the story was mere repetition.

Dawlish tucked the newspaper under his arm. After all, it was nothing really to do with him. Why should he bother? All Felicity had asked was for confirmation of the rumour, but somehow he felt sorry for the old man and interested in the burglary.

He paid off the taxi and hurried into the club, hoping that Pop would still be there. He was—in the same chair with a whisky-and-soda in front of him. Catching sight of Dawlish he beckoned him over for a drink.

'That's very nice of you,' said Dawlish, sitting down. He put his 'evening' newspaper on the table, so that by leaning forward Pop could see part of the headline. The old man was not interested, however. He gave Dawlish the impression that he wanted to say something but did not quite know where to begin.

'Ah, here's your drink.' He raised his own glass. 'To a good holiday!' he toasted.

'Thanks very much,' said Dawlish. 'I—'

He stopped speaking as a young man hurried towards them, a newspaper in his hand.

Pop put down his glass sharply.

'Now what do *you* want?' he growled at the newcomer.

'Have you seen *this*?' the other demanded, thrusting the newspaper into his hand. Pop glanced with some distaste towards the newcomer. The visitor was agitated, and his hands were unsteady as he took out a cigarette case and lighter.

Pop's eyes moved indifferently back to the paper; then his hands gripped it with sudden alarm as he flung it agitatedly aside.

'How is she?'

'I don't now,' replied the newcomer. 'I thought you—'

'Why the devil didn't you find out from the hospital before coming here?' demanded Fairweather. He rose from his chair and strode purposefully towards the door, barking out a peremptory order to the young man to stay where he was.

Dawlish waited until Pop had gone, and then asked mildly:

'Would you care for a drink?'

'Eh? Oh, no thanks. Too early.' The young man looked at him for the first time. 'I—er—I'm afraid my uncle is rather upset.'

Dawlish picked up the paper and re-read the headlines.

'Nasty affair,' he commented, and beckoned the steward. 'Coffee for one,' he ordered.

He noticed that the young man's eyes were troubled. Dawlish had heard vaguely of Pop's nephew; the incident gave him some idea of the difficulty of serving the old man.

The coffee arrived and Dawlish poured out. His companion drank distractedly, his attention clearly fixed on his uncle's return.

When at last he came, the young man was ordered at once to fetch a taxi.

'I've kept mine waiting,' he replied. 'I didn't think you'd want to lose any time.'

'Really Richard—why on earth didn't you tell me?' demanded Pop, irascibly. 'Come along, then. You'll excuse us, Dawlish, won't you?'

'By all means,' Dawlish said, standing up.

He watched their departure with some amusement; it would not be long before a storm blew up between uncle and nephew.

Waiting just long enough for them to have left the club, Dawlish took a taxi to the *Cafe Royal,* arriving a little after half past twelve. He expected to find that Ted Beresford and Tim Jeremy, who was to have made a third, had left. But he found them sitting at a table in the bar.

Tim was the first to speak.

'I shall inform Felicity,' he announced.

'That's good,' said Dawlish. 'What about?'

'That at the first opportunity you not only stand Ted and me up, but go dashing off after the talk of the town.'

Dawlish grinned.

'It was Felicity who put me on to her,' he said, as he sat down. 'I suppose you've been too busy drinking beer to make inquiries.'

'No one needs to make inquiries,' declared Tim. 'The world knows all there is to know about Georgette. If you lived in London—'

Dawlish pulled his chair forward.

'As I don't, you can have the enormous satisfaction of putting me wise. Who is she going to marry, for instance?'

Ted Beresford started.

'Marry?'

'She never does,' said Tim, sitting down.

'That's the one thing in her favour,' remarked Ted.

'Yet Paris is agog with the story of her latest engagement,' murmured Dawlish, with some exaggeration, 'and Felicity was so fussed about it, that she wrote and asked me to make inquiries.'

Ted rubbed his chin thoughtfully.

'When you feel inclined, tell us what all this is about,' he invited.

'Do you mean to say that Felicity is worried about *Georgette*?' questioned Tim.

'She's worried about Georgette's newest victim, who was a friend of her father's,' Dawlish said. 'It may be that he is beginning to doubt the wisdom of letting his heart rule his head. I shall be surprised if Georgette, sensing this, hasn't pulled a fast one—'

'Now steady!' protested Ted.

Dawlish chuckled.

'Oh, it's a guess, I admit.'

'That Georgette is prepared to arrange a burglary?' scoffed Tim. 'Be your age!'

'No one in their right senses would burgle Georgette's flat,' Dawlish asserted. 'It's fairly well known that her jewels are as phoney as her virtue. What's more no thief would burgle so late in the morning, at a time when people are astir.'

'How do you know what time the burglary was committed?' demanded Ted. 'It isn't in the papers.'

'Well, she was found unconscious about eight o'clock but her condition isn't serious,' Dawlish said. 'If she'd been attacked in the early hours, but not seriously hurt, she wouldn't still be unconscious at eight o'clock. Therefore, it looks as if she were 'attacked' a short while before the maid came in—which isn't likely—or that she wasn't really unconscious.'

Ted looked at Tim.

'He's off again,' remarked Tim, sadly.

'Wild guessing,' said Ted, severely.

'I'll give you two to one that the police aren't satisfied with their findings,' Dawlish offered. 'Georgette thought the best way of working on the old boy was to show herself as a poor, helpless woman, needing a man's protection. Judging from his mood this morning, he's likely to fall for it, too,' Dawlish added.

'You haven't told us who he is yet,' said Tim, sharply.

'None other than Pop Fairweather,' announced Dawlish.

'She's taking a big chance,' remarked Tim, selecting a piece of cheese with passionate interest. 'If Pop ever discovered that she had put one across him, that would put paid to her hopes.'

'How can he discover that?' asked Ted.

'He might be informed,' Dawlish observed. 'He made it pretty clear that the match isn't regarded with any favour by his friends, and that probably includes his relatives. But there's one thing that rather puzzles me.'

'Indeed? How modest!'

'Why,' continued Dawlish, completely unruffled, 'has Georgette, who had managed very nicely on her own up to now, suddenly chosen to marry an old man? Because he might die soon, leaving her a fortune? Possibly—but Pop's the type who seems likely to become a nonagenarian. So why doesn't she choose someone nearer her own age?'

He stopped talking, his face set in the wooden, closed-in expression which in him denoted intense concentration.

After a pause, he went on musingly: 'I find it hard to believe that Georgette would think of such a trick herself—it suggests to me that someone else is in the background. Now Pop is a man of some importance and a power in the world of steel and commerce. There are possibilities in this business, chaps. Are either of you very busy?'

Tim said: 'I'm not.'

'I'm on leave,' Ted said.

'Excellent.' Dawlish leaned forward with a beaming smile. 'You're in the city, Tim. Find out if any rumours are being passed round, will you?'

'And what about me?' asked Ted.

'You might find out where Pop's nephew, Richard, spends his leisure, and strike up an acquaintance with him,' suggested Dawlish. 'I think that young man is feeling a bit blue and hard-done-by. A perfect condition for interesting developments.'

'What are *you* going to do?' demanded Tim, challengingly.

Dawlish grinned.

'I'll ask Bill Trivett if he'd like to make a foursome for dinner tonight. He'll know if there are grounds for suspecting any monkey-business about this burglary.'

'I am on,' said Tim. 'I like old Trivett. Where shall we dine?'

'*Arbutt's*, I think,' said Dawlish after a moment's consideration. 'That's a nice reputable place where a Scotland Yard Superintendent won't mind being seen. Seven-thirty,' he added briskly. 'Now I'd better get back to the club, Pop is probably just finishing his lunch.'

He left his friends in Regent Street, and as they watched his huge figure crossing the road, Ted chuckled.

'He's as deep as ever,' Tim remarked.

'Deeper,' declared Ted. 'The odd thing is that he's almost certainly right, too. We might have a busy week ahead,' he continued, cheerfully. 'I'll see you tonight.'

CHAPTER THREE

TRIVETT OF THE YARD

Scotland Yard is a repository of secrets, of odd little snippets of information which seem unimportant when they are brought in, but which often prove useful later on.

Of late, there had been vague talk about Georgette Lee and some of her new friends, one or two of whom greatly interested the police. When the report came through about the burglary, therefore, it received much more attention than it would have done in the ordinary course of events.

Among the senior officials at the Yard who took notice, was Superintendent William Trivett.

The initial stages of the inquiry were not considered important enough for the attention of a Superintendent, and Detective Sergeant Hardy had been along to Georgette's flat with a detective officer; from here, they had gone to the hospital to question Georgette.

Hardy had finished his part by midday and after reporting, went to the canteen, where he talked freely among his friends about the case.

Trivett went out to lunch. When he returned Detective Inspector Munk, his chief *aide,* a broad, fierce-looking man with an abrupt manner and a bristling moustache, was sitting in his office.

'Anything come in?' Trivett asked.

'Nothing that matters,' said Munk. 'Not that it would have made much difference.'

'What do you mean?' asked Trivett.

'Well, you weren't here, were you?' demanded Munk. 'If you'd gone to the canteen you'd have heard plenty.'

'About Georgette?'

'Certainly about Georgette. Hardy was down there, shooting his mouth off as usual. It's a pity he doesn't know when to keep quiet.' Munk's voice was both righteous and aggrieved. 'He says he thinks it was phoney. The door was opened with a key, although there's supposed to be only two, Georgette's and the maid's. And she was hardly hurt at all.' Munk sniffed. 'Insurance racket, I shouldn't wonder.'

'Georgette wouldn't try an old one like that,' said Trivett, 'especially when she's got Fairweather on a piece of string.'

'You never know what they'll try,' Munk opined, 'the old man may have turned her down and she may be desperate for cash.'

'What else did Hardy say?' asked Trivett.

'There wasn't any sign of Fairweather,' Munk told him. 'If you ask me,' he added darkly, 'she's lost him and is trying to get a bit of money put by. You needn't tell me she doesn't know that she's on the way out. Being pally with a man like Len Morgan is proof enough of that. How I'd like to get something on that crooked devil! Anything special for me to do this afternoon?'

Munk left the office a little after three o'clock, and as he did so, the telephone bell rang.

'Mr. Patrick Dawlish would like a word with you,' said the Yard operator.

'Oh—put him through . . . Hallo, Pat,' said Trivett, with some warmth. 'How are you?'

'Fairly well, considering Felicity's in Paris,' Dawlish answered, cheerfully. 'I'm going to *Arbutt's* with Ted and Tim tonight. Are you free?'

'Tonight? I think so,' said Trivett, and looked in his diary. 'Yes, I can manage it. Thanks. What time?'

'Half past seven,' said Dawlish. 'That's fine, Bill. How's crime?'

'Well under control, thanks,' said Trivett, drily.

As he hung up the receiver, he reflected that Dawlish more often than not had an ulterior motive for telephoning him, but he could think of nothing which might be attracting his attention just now.

Trivett had a great respect for the big man's perspicacity and powers of deduction. Dawlish had a knack of cutting through inessentials and getting to the root of any mystery which engaged his attention. He had at one time served with Intelligence, and become a sensational figure in several violent affrays, Beresford and Jeremy working with him.

Trivett gave very little thought to Georgette Lee for the rest of that afternoon.

Before the dinner party, Tim Jeremy told Dawlish that there were no rumours about Fairweather's activities in the City; and Ted Beresford complained that Richard Lloyd appeared to have no leisure whatever. He was a member of two clubs, but seldom visited either of them; he was reputed to be a slave to the old man.

When Trivett arrived, the subject was dropped; but before the evening was over, Dawlish and his friends knew that the police believed that the burglary had been faked. They also knew that Georgette Lee had admitted that the stolen jewels were of little value, and that only a small sum of money had been taken.

* * *

The next morning Pop Fairweather parked his Rolls Royce outside a house in Chelsea. He walked up the short drive, and opened the front door with a latch key. The house was fully furnished, and he made a complete tour of it, nodding his approval over the things which pleased him and shaking his head over those which did not. When he finished, he rang up the firm of house agents who had given him the keys.

An obsequious young man answered his call.

'I will take the house as it stands,' said Pop, 'and I shall want possession immediately.'

'Certainly, sir. I will have the agreement made out this afternoon and sent round to your office, if that is in order, sir.'

'It isn't in order,' growled Pop. 'I will come to you and sign it. Have it ready by half past four.'

He banged down the receiver, and as he did so, caught sight of a man who was coming in through the gate—a little shabby man who approached the front door with uncertain steps and then shuffled away.

At the rattle of the letter-box Pop expected to see a circular lying on the mat; instead, there was a letter. He picked it up, surprised to see that it was addressed to *N. Fairweather, Esq.*

In some wonderment he tore the envelope open, perturbed because, as far as he was aware, no one but the house agents knew that he contemplated buying this house.

He stiffened suddenly as he read the words:

How much do you think Georgie paid to arrange that burglary? 'Burglary'!' Don't make me laugh! She couldn't think of a better way of making you come up to scratch.

The words were written in block capitals and there was no signature.

He opened the front door and hurried towards the gate, but long before he reached it, the shabby individual who had delivered the letter was out of sight. A policeman was passing on the other side of the street and, seeing the white-bearded and obviously angry man, crossed the road.

'Anything I can do, sir?'

Pop looked into a round red face and a pair of shrewd grey eyes. He frowned.

'Did you see the man who came to my house?' he demanded.

'*Your* house?' asked the constable. 'I thought—'

'Yes, *my* house. I've just bought it. Did you see that man?' reiterated Pop.

'I saw a man go in at the gate,' said the policeman. 'Nothing wrong, is there, sir?'

Pop stared at him.

'No,' he said, in a milder voice. 'Thank you, Constable.' He nodded, and went back to the house.

He had intended to leave immediately; instead he went into the drawing-room, looking out of the window on to the trim lawn. Those who knew the old man well would have guessed that he was thinking very deeply—and that he was in a quandary.

Pop stood brooding for over twenty minutes before he made a move. Then he slammed the front door behind him, climbed into the Rolls and drove off without looking behind him.

A quarter of an hour after leaving Chelsea he was standing in the small, austere hall at Scotland Yard, where casual visitors were received.

In Trivett's office, Munk was sitting at his desk, writing a report, when the telephone bell rang. He frowned, and lifted the receiver.

'Munk speaking . . . Eh . . .' He listened intently, glancing round at Trivett. 'Old man Fairweather's called about the burglary, and wants to see the inspector in charge. Interested?' barked Munk.

'Fairweather?' Trivett showed his surprise. 'Yes, I'll see him, have him sent along.'

It would be the first time he had met Fairweather.

He liked the old man on sight. The trim white beard and penetrating gaze appealed to him. He stood up to welcome the caller, motioning to an easy chair.

Quite unimpressed, Pop settled himself into it. He said sharply:

'I understand that you are Superintendent Trivett—what is there about the burglary that demands *your* attention, Mr. Trivett?'

'The case is under my supervision,' Trivett explained.

'I see. Do you know who broke into the flat?'

'I'm afraid we don't,' confessed Trivett.

'Any chance of finding him?' demanded Pop.

'There's always a chance,' said Trivett, reasoningly, 'although I will be frank and admit that we haven't any inkling of the identity of the burglar, Mr. Fairweather. The door was opened by a key, the man obviously wearing gloves. The most likely way of finding him will be through the missing articles though, as they were of no great value, they may never be put on the market.'

'Can you find out who stole the key?'

Trivett leaned back in his chair, the slight frown of concentration on his handsome face giving him a look of maturity beyond his years.

'I don't think a key was stolen,' he said at last. 'It's much more likely that one was removed at some time from the maid's or Miss Lee's bag, and that an impression of it was taken and a key cut from that impression. Neither Miss Lee nor her maid have missed their keys.'

Fairweather sat erect, and squared his shoulders.

'Mr. Trivett, I want you to answer my question frankly. *Was* there a burglary at Miss Lee's flat?'

Trivett, taken by surprise, stammered: 'I—er—I don't quite know what you mean.'

He felt as if he had been caught out in a simple confidence trick, and the frosty glint in the old man's eye reminded him of a magistrate about to deal with an incorrigible vagrant.

'I see,' said Pop, grimly. 'You have reason to doubt it, Mr. Trivett. I will not take up more of your valuable time.' He stood up, inclined his head, and reached the door before Trivett had fully recovered.

'Mr. Fairweather, I must ask you—'

'I have all the information I require, thank you,' said Pop. 'Good-day to you.'

He strode along the passage, his footsteps resounding clearly on the stone floor.

An hour later the young man in the estate agent's office answered the telephone promptly. His greeting to Nathaniel Fairweather rang out cheerfully; negotiations for the sales of expensive houses did not often go through so easily as the one for the house in Chelsea.

As he replaced the receiver, however, his expression was one of dismay; he was not even in time to stop the typist from finishing the contract of the cancelled sale.

CHAPTER FOUR

A SHOCK FOR GEORGETTE

The next day was a trying one for Georgette; by the middle of the afternoon she was genuinely exhausted. Soon after breakfast the telephone bell had rung with the first of the solicitous inquiries after her health, and had been ringing ever since.

To make it worse, her maid had a cold.

Every time the girl came into the room, she sniffed.

Pop had not called.

Georgette was not seriously troubled by that, although she had been expecting to hear from him.

She sat, now with her feet resting on a silk-covered stool, an illustrated magazine open on her lap. Being 'convalescent' she was wearing a salmon-pink negligee frilled with cobwebby lace. Few women of forty-three would have risked wearing such a garment, but Georgette, her hair a golden glory, was able to carry it off. Hers was not a chocolate-box beauty, there was character in her face and determination in her expression.

She heard the front door bell ring, and felt sure that the caller was Pop.

The maid opened the door.

'It's Mr. Lloyd, Miss,' she said, and sniffed.

As she spoke Richard Lloyd, stepping past her, hurried into the room. He closed the door on the sniffing girl and stood still, looking at Georgette, whose disappointment was now touched with dismay.

'Richard, what on earth's brought you here?'

Lloyd moved forward slowly.

'I've come because I've got to make one more attempt to stop you. Georgette, you can't go on with this, it's absolutely crazy.'

'Richard, please!'

'And I'm not going to be put off with a few kind words,' said Lloyd. 'Georgette, can't you see what you're doing? To marry an old man like Uncle Nathaniel—why, it's madness!'

Georgette kept her voice steady.

'We've had all this out before,' she said, 'and I haven't changed my mind.'

'I don't intend to take that as final.'

'It is final,' insisted Georgette.

The anger which she had felt when he had first come in had quite gone. She saw from his expression that he was in a dangerously serious mood; dangerous enough to upset her plans. She thought quickly; the best way to manage him would be by appearing friendly and sympathetic—a quarrel would only make him more obstinate.

'Come and sit down,' she said, 'and—'

'I'll stand, thanks.' He stared at her, his frown darkening. 'It wouldn't last a month! You've no idea what he's really like. There are two sides to my uncle, and—'

'I think I know both sides,' Georgette said, 'and you've warned me often enough. Do sit down, Richard.'

He hesitated, then obeyed; she had won the first round.

Lloyd sat still and erect; his eyes held a look which she had seen in the eyes of other young men. She was not to be blamed because so many became infatuated with her; and she had perfected the art of refusing their proposals without hurting them. But so far Richard Lloyd had been proof against that art.

'Richard,' she began, earnestly, 'I know Pop's a lot older than I am, but we've much the same personalities. No, it's no use shaking your head! You may know Pop in all his moods, but you've only seen one side of me. And you're not quite right about my age, you know—I'm more than half again as old as you.'

'Nonsense!'

'How old are you, Richard?'

'That's got nothing to do with it. I—'

'You're twenty-seven, aren't you?' she asked. 'I'm in the early forties. It's no more absurd for me to think of marrying Pop than it is for you to think of marrying me, except that Pop and I have both reached the stage when we want to settle down to a quiet life and you—well, your life's in front of you. Richard—' she leaned forward impressively—'supposing I were to marry you. When you're forty, I'll be nearly *sixty*. Doesn't that make you think?'

She had startled him, but he shrugged his shoulders impatiently.

'You're pretending because—'

'That's the truth,' she insisted. 'I haven't any illusions, you know. In a few years I'll be no longer beautiful, I shall be an elderly woman quite content to look after Pop. I certainly shan't want to keep up the pace that a man of your age would set.'

She paused, and this time he did not answer. She had not spoken so bluntly to him before, and it was obvious that she had given him cause to think. She hesitated, undecided whether to press her advantage or to allow him to speak next, when the front door bell rang.

Lloyd said abruptly: 'Whoever it is, don't see them, Georgette. I'm going to have this out, and it's no use thinking that you can fool me. The gap in our ages doesn't matter, and if it's money you're worried about, I've plenty. In a few years time I shall inherit much more. I—'

He broke off.

He knew that she was no longer listening to him; she was staring at the door, with a tense expression, as it slowly opened. He glanced over his shoulder, then saw his uncle standing there.

Pop shot him a quick, searing glance.

'Georgette, I want a word with you, outside.'

'Why darling, of course.'

Pop looked at her unsmilingly.

She thought she knew him well; only now did she realize that she was seeing for the first time one of the moods to which Richard had referred. Without a change of manner she walked to the door, which Pop held open, and then closed behind them.

'Oh, I'm so glad you've come,' she cried confidently. 'I've tried to keep this from you, but Richard—'

'We will not discuss my nephew,' said Pop, abruptly. 'I've come to tell you that we shall not be seeing each other again, Georgette.'

'*Pop!*' She looked at him with startled eyes.

'And I have not come to argue the point,' said Pop in a harsh, emotionless voice, 'but I will tell you why I have come to this decision. The burglary here was a fake. It was arranged for my benefit. I was to be so alarmed by your danger, that I would marry you forthwith. If that isn't enough,' went on Fairweather, 'there is another reason. A little secret of yours which—but never mind. You know what I mean.'

'But . . .'

'I have settled twenty thousand pounds on you,' Fairweather went on, ignoring her. 'You will receive the interest during my lifetime and the capital sum at my death. This settlement should amply compensate you for your broken heart and spoiled plans.'

'Pop, please—' Georgette began.

He turned away and went out.

Georgette was unaware of the lounge door opening and Lloyd standing watching her; he was so appalled by her expression that at first he could not make a move.

Steeling himself, he went forward at last, and touched her shoulder.

'Georgette, my dear—'

She swung round.

'Get out!' she cried. 'Get out, you bleating young fool, I hate the sight of you. Get out!'

She turned on him, driving him towards the door. Taken aback he made no serious effort to resist her. In a whirl of fury she flung the door open.

'Whatever happens, Georgette, I love you. If you ever need help—'

'*Get out!*'

She slammed the door behind him, and burst into tears.

News of the break between Georgette and Pop reached Dawlish two days afterwards.

He telephoned Ted and Tim, learning from Ted that Richard Lloyd was supposed to have quarrelled with his uncle, and had left the Company's offices in the middle of the afternoon—he had not yet returned and, according to rumours, he was no longer working for the old man.

'. . . so your fears can be set at rest,' Dawlish wrote to Felicity, 'the beauty has failed to snare the beast and Pop will continue to sit in his favourite chair in the club every morning.

'When are you coming home?'

Felicity's reply was a telephone call. Joan Beresford had caught summer 'flu, and though there was no cause for anxiety, she would probably be confined to bed for at least a week. And:

'I *can't* very well leave her, Pat,' said Felicity.

'Of course you can't,' agreed Dawlish, 'but I may come over for the week-end—'

'Do try,' urged Felicity. 'My holiday hasn't worked out at all as I expected.' She gave a little laugh. 'And if you had plunged into some mystery, I should never have forgiven myself.'

'The danger of that is quite over,' Dawlish assured her.

At that very moment, Pop Fairweather was lying on the floor of his nephew's bedroom, with his head bloody and battered. He was unconscious; and when Richard Lloyd entered the room and found him, the old man appeared to be dead.

CHAPTER FIVE

AN AFFAIR OF VIOLENCE

Dawlish was asleep.

He slept on his back, with his lips tightly closed, breathing easily and softly. He had come in late after a session with Tim and Ted, during which they had mourned the fact that the affair of Pop Fairweather had ended so tamely.

Something woke Dawlish. He couldn't be sure what the sound had been.

'Excuse me, sir,' a man's voice murmured from the door.

Dawlish grunted.

'It's the night porter, sir. I knocked but you didn't hear. May I put on the light?'

Dawlish gave a vague sound of assent.

'I'm very sorry to disturb you, sir, but there's a gentleman downstairs who says that he must see you. His name's Lloyd.'

'Lloyd?' echoed Dawlish.

'Mr. Richard Lloyd. He says you know him. He looks rather upset, sir, I might say *considerably* upset.'

'Drunk?' inquired Dawlish, throwing back the bedclothes. His thoughts flew from the nephew to the uncle.

'I wouldn't say that, sir.'

'I'll come down,' said Dawlish. 'Take him into the smoking-room—that's empty, isn't it?'

'It's bound to be now, it's after a half past two. Shall I bring you anything, sir?'

'A cup of tea would be welcome,' said Dawlish.

When the porter had gone, Dawlish plunged his face into cold water and dressed rapidly.

The club was gloomy by night. Only a few dim lights were on, and they threw shadows on the landing. The lift seemed to make noise enough to wake the dead, but when Dawlish closed the gates behind him, a hush fell upon the building.

Arriving in the hall, he hesitated for a moment outside the glass door. He could see Lloyd pacing up and down, smoking nervously. Undoubtedly the young man was extremely agitated.

Dawlish went into him.

Lloyd sprang forward.

'I wouldn't have disturbed you at this hour if it hadn't been urgent, Major Dawlish,' he said, showing that in spite of his agitation he had himself well under control. 'I remembered that my uncle said you were staying here and I've come to you because I think you may be able to help me.'

'If I can,' murmured Dawlish.

Lloyd swallowed rapidly.

'My uncle was brutally assaulted during the night, and is now in hospital. He is undergoing an emergency operation to save his life.'

'I'm very sorry to hear that,' said Dawlish, slowly.

'He was in my flat at the time,' Lloyd went on, 'and I arrived some time after the attack—how long after I don't know.' He gave Dawlish the impression that in spite of the gravity of his news, he had not yet come to the real point. 'It's not only a question of finding out who assaulted my uncle, if it were as straightforward as that I would have left it in the hands of the police, but—they have made an arrest.'

'Oh,' said Dawlish, evenly. 'Who's the man?'

'It isn't a man,' said Richard Lloyd, 'it's Georgette Lee.'

Once he had broken that news, Lloyd was almost embarrassingly frank; if Dawlish were going to help, he said, obviously everything must be told. So Dawlish soon learned that uncle and nephew had been suitors of Georgette, and Lloyd described the encounter in Georgette's flat.

Later, there had been a flare-up between Lloyd and his uncle; as a result, Lloyd had resigned from his directorship of *Fairweather, Field & Fairweather* and also from his position as private secretary to the old man.

'I didn't know that he was coming to see me,' Lloyd went on. 'Not being in a mood for my own company I'd gone out for a drink. I must have been gone from perhaps half past eight until ten o'clock. When I came back, I saw that the bedroom light was on. I went in to switch it off, and found my uncle—'

He broke off. Dawlish made no comment.

'It was a grim sight,' Lloyd went on at last. 'He's been battered about the head pretty badly. He was lying on his face, and I should say that he'd been attacked from behind. It gave me a hell of a shock.'

'Of course,' agreed Dawlish.

'I rang up the police and they were at the flat within twenty minutes. I sent for a doctor, too. I had no time to look about much and I noticed little, but soon after the police arrived they found a handkerchief—Georgette's,' he added, abruptly.

'Did you identify it yourself?' asked Dawlish.

'Yes, and I haven't forgiven myself,' snapped Lloyd.

'My dear chap, there's nothing to reproach yourself with,' Dawlish said, 'the first principle when dealing with the police is to tell the truth, without worrying about its implications. And on the strength of the handkerchief, they arrested Georgette?'

'No, that wasn't all,' said Lloyd. 'She had been at the flat during the evening—she left a note for me. I didn't see that, either, but the police found it.'

'Did she have a key to your flat?'

Lloyd flushed.

'As a matter of fact, she did. Look here, Dawlish, you needn't think there was anything like *that,* I do assure you there wasn't.'

'I see,' murmured Dawlish. 'And did your uncle also have a key?'

'Oh, yes,' said Lloyd. 'He didn't like it because I refused to go on living in his house. I couldn't go on with it. He used to drag me out of bed to discuss some pet scheme of his in the middle of the night, and I hardly got a wink of sleep. When I took the flat, he sold up his house, and came to live here, but he insisted on having a key to my flat so that he could get in at any time.'

'Since you've moved you've had a fair amount of leis-sure?' asked Dawlish.

Lloyd gave a short laugh.

'What a hope! You'd be astonished at the number of different interests the old man's got. I provide the work, and he provides—or thinks he does—the brains.'

'And doesn't he?' asked Dawlish.

'He's no fool,' conceded Lloyd grudgingly, 'but he's not so clever as he thinks he is. But that doesn't affect the present situation.' Lloyd's tone hardened. 'My uncle probably came to see me hoping to persuade me to change my mind about working for him, and was attacked while he was there. There isn't any doubt that Georgette was also at the flat, but for the police to think that she would knock him about like that—oh, it's absurd! I doubt if she has the strength, for one thing.'

'Some women are deceptively strong,' said Dawlish.

'If you knew Georgette, you'd know there isn't a chance that she would do it,' snapped Lloyd. 'Dawlish, you remember when I came here the other morning to see my uncle?'

'Yes.'

'He said that if ever he were in a spot and wanted help, he wouldn't hesitate to come to you. Now—well, you will help, won't you?'

'I'll try to find out whether the case against Miss Lee really seems to stand up,' Dawlish said. 'What about this note that was left for you?'

Lloyd did not immediately answer. He took out cigarettes, lit one absently and stared at Dawlish without appearing to see him. Undoubtedly there was a picture of Georgette in his mind's eye. His lips were set tightly, and his face looked much older than when Dawlish had first seen him.

He began to speak in a low-pitched voice.

'That's the worst feature of the whole business,' he said. 'I'd told Georgette that if ever I could help her, she had only to ask me. And the note said something like this: "I'm going to need help badly, Richard".' Lloyd paused, then went on hotly: 'It must have been forged. If the police are in their right senses, surely they know that she wouldn't have left a note like that, if she'd attacked the old man.'

'They might think that she wrote the note first, and was surprised by your uncle,' Dawlish said. 'If she did attack him—'

'I tell you that's impossible!'

Dawlish stood up abruptly.

'Now look here, Lloyd, we've got to be realists about this business. It isn't impossible. It may not be likely and it certainly doesn't sound in character, but your uncle had just turned her down, hadn't he? And for some time she had reason to think that they were going to get married.'

'Oh, don't give me any of this "woman spurned" business,' cried Lloyd.

Dawlish shrugged.

'Truth can be terribly trite and hackneyed. You must face the possibility of a quarrel in which in a fit of rage she could have gone for him. He is an old man, while she's a comparatively young woman.'

'He's as strong as a horse! Why, he would have floored her in no time.'

'Possibly,' Dawlish said, 'but she could have clubbed him when his back was turned, and you're not going to help anyone by pretending that she couldn't. Still, some features make it seem unlikely—the note for one, also that she made no attempt to hide the fact that she had been to see you. The police will realize that as well as we do,' he added. 'By midday I shall probably be able to tell you how strong a case they have against Georgette.'

'I'll be very grateful,' Lloyd said, 'but—Dawlish, whatever you or anyone else may think, I'm quite sure in my own mind that Georgette didn't do it. Will you help me?'

'I'll help you if I think the police have got hold of the wrong end of the stick,' Dawlish promised. 'Meanwhile there's a job for you,' he added cheerfully.

'What's that?' demanded Lloyd eagerly.

'If you're so sure that Georgette's innocent, try to think of someone who may be guilty,' Dawlish said. 'All attacks have motives behind them! As you handle all your uncle's affairs, you may know of someone who has a reason to wish him dead.'

After a pause, Lloyd said: 'I know a lot of people who haven't much love for him, but I can't say that I know of anyone who would go quite so far as to attempt to murder him.' He hesitated before he went on: 'But I'll think about it, although I'm afraid we'll have to start from scratch. There's one point on which you want putting right though—the old man keeps a lot to himself. He certainly doesn't tell me everything.'

'Then there's your lead,' Dawlish said promptly. 'While he's in hospital, find out all you can about the business he keeps from you.'

'You seem to take it for granted that he'll recover,' Lloyd said. 'Judging from what they said at the hospital, he hasn't much chance.'

'That needn't stop you investigating,' Dawlish said.

'I suppose not. Where shall I meet you?'

'I think this is as good a place as any,' Dawlish suggested. 'We can talk upstairs in my room. Let's make it half past twelve, shall we, and we can have some lunch afterwards.'

'Right-ho,' said Lloyd, and added a little awkwardly: 'Thanks very much, Dawlish. I'm sorry I dragged you out of bed like this.'

'Forget it,' murmured Dawlish, and led the way out of the smoking-room to the front door.

Lloyd climbed into a red two-seater, turning to wave as he drove off.

Dawlish stood on the porch watching the departing car. A little flash of light caught his eye, from the other side of the road. He dismissed it from his mind as the sports car neared Admiralty Arch, for another car, its headlights blazing, suddenly swung straight in its path.

He saw the red two-seater twist up on to the pavement. Then it was back in the road and, in the bright headlights, he could make out figures hurrying through the Arch and guessed that the police were on the spot. The headlights went out suddenly.

CHAPTER SIX

MAN OF ACTION

Dawlish had started to run to the scene of the crash when he saw the figure of a man detach itself from the shadow of a tree on the opposite side of the Mall and scurry towards St. James's Park. There was something furtive about the man's movements, and Dawlish remembered the little point of light that had caught his eye as Lloyd drove off. An idea flashed into his mind and he darted across the Mall in pursuit.

He saw his quarry on the path ahead of him passing beneath a lamp. Dawlish put on a spurt, and the man, hearing his footsteps ran too. He reached the Park, and plunged out of sight among some stunted may-trees.

Dawlish reached the group of trees and stood listening. Not far away he could hear the sound of heavy breathing. He moved forward stealthily, his footsteps muffled by the grass. In front of him was a stack of garden chairs, and the chances were that the man was on the far side of it.

He took a good grip on the chairs nearest him and with a tremendous heave sent the whole pile over. There was a crash and a cry.

Dawlish leapt forward, as his quarry struggled to rise.

He jerked the man upright, shining a torch full in his face. It was a broad, ugly, frightened face.

'Let me go—you bastard!' muttered the man, and tugged weakly at his arm.

'Such a scared little man,' mused Dawlish, towering over him. 'Do you happen to have a name?'

'You—you've no right—'

'Of course I haven't,' said Dawlish promptly, 'I've committed assault and battery without the slightest provocation. That's a thought, we'll go along to the police and you can make a charge. Shall we start walking?' He pushed the man in front of him, still holding his arm, forcing him to go towards the Mall.

The man swung round.

'Let me go, you—'

'But we haven't seen the policeman,' protested Dawlish. 'Of course, if you'd really like to go without seeing one, I don't mind. But you'd have to tell me the truth first. You were watching my friend's car, weren't you?'

'What car?'

'The little red one, parked in the Mall,' Dawlish went on. 'You were stationed by that tree and the moment the red car moved off, you signalled to someone in the Arch, who passed the signal on to the man in the car. Isn't that true?'

'It's a lie!'

'You don't sound very convincing,' murmured Dawlish. 'How much were you paid for the job?'

'I never did any job. Leave me—why, you—'

Dawlish swung the man round, and thrust a hand deep into the pocket of the threadbare coat. His fingers closed over a wad of notes, and drew them out. There were twenty or thirty at least, and he looked at them thoughtfully. It was remarkable, to say the least, that such a shabby little man should have so much money.

'Blood money?' asked Dawlish. The bantering note had left his voice, and the words came crisp and hard. 'You were watching the car, weren't you?'

'What if I was?' whined the other. 'There's no crime in that, is there?'

'And he paid you twenty odd pounds,' rasped Dawlish.

'He—'

'What's it to be? The truth, or an interview with the police?'

'I never knew what he was going to do. I did one or two jobs for him. But there wasn't any harm in them.'

'Tell me about them,' commanded Dawlish.

The man was willing enough to talk. Dawlish read his mind easily; he was scared because of the attempt to crash Lloyd's car and knew that if he were caught by the police, things would probably go hard with him. He obviously had a police record, and now considered that to fall in with Dawlish's demands would be his best chance.

His mouth set in a thin line and crafty look came into his eyes.

'What'd it be worth to you to know?' he said.

'A quid a job,' answered Dawlish promptly.

'On the level?'

'On the level,' said Dawlish.

'Well, the first job I did was watching a house to see who called on the lady. Name of Lee.'

'And who did call?' asked Dawlish.

'The old boy, Fairweather, and his nephew Lloyd.'

'And what were the other jobs?' Dawlish asked him.

'I had to drop a letter into a house where Fairweather went one day last week, and skip.'

'And where was this house?'

'Middleton Street, Chelsea—number 9.'

'And what else?' asked Dawlish.

'I took a few messages.'

'Where to?'

'I had to take one to Piccadilly and give it to a chap who asked for it—wore a red ribbon in my buttonhole so's he'd recognize me. There was one at Charing Cross Station, another at Victoria.'

'I see. And what about tonight?'

The man hesitated and then mumbled: 'I had to flash a torch when the red car moved off. That's all, I swear.'

'Then we'll call it a fiver,' Dawlish said cheerfully, drawing out his wallet. 'And now, would you like to make some *more* money?'

'If it's clean,' said the man unctuously.

'It'll be as clean as any you're likely to handle,' remarked Dawlish. 'Where can I get hold of you?'

'I've a bed at Joe Speller's doss house in the Mile End Road most nights. They all know me there—Bert May, that's my name,' he added, with a grin doubtless inspired by the notes which Dawlish was handing to him. 'Any time you want me I'll pick up a message at Joe Speller's. You can't miss Joe's.'

'We haven't quite finished,' Dawlish said, laying a detaining hand on the other's arm. 'What are you going to do about your friend who paid you for tonight's job?'

'Nothing,' declared Bert virtuously. 'I've finished with him.'

'I don't think you should,' said Dawlish, gently.

Bert stared.

'Do what he asks and don't argue about it unless it looks as if it will lead to serious trouble,' Dawlish said, 'but remember that every job you do I want to hear about.'

'I get you,' said Bert, with a sly grin. 'Okay—I'll be on my way.' He gave an airy wave of the hand and shuffled off in the direction of Buckingham Palace.

Dawlish watched him as he disappeared.

The man's story contained much information which might be useful and Dawlish blessed his luck for having spotted him. He walked quickly back towards Trafalgar Square, but the road was deserted. There was a bad skid mark near the kerb, and some scattering of broken glass; otherwise there was no indication of an accident. He half-expected to find Lloyd waiting for him at the club, but the night porter had not seen the young man since Dawlish had left.

Dawlish pondered over the night's events while he was undressing. Not until he was in bed did he remember that he was supposed to be booking a seat on an air-liner to Paris for the week-end.

He was awake just before eight o'clock. As each bedroom at the Carilon was fitted with a telephone, he made a call to the Westminster hospital before his tea arrived. An impersonal voice told him that the operation on Mr. Fairweather had been successful but that the patient's condition remained grave.

Then he rang up Trivett, who told him that the Fairweather case was fixed for ten o'clock, at Marlborough Street.

'So I haven't much time,' Dawlish murmured to himself, as he rang off.

He washed and shaved quickly, and was in the breakfast room at twenty minutes to nine. At ten past, he telephoned Airways House, and was told that there were no seats on the Paris plane until the next weekend. He telegraphed Felicity, saying: *Nothing doing, sorry darling, hope Joan's better,* and hoped that she would not be worried when she heard what had happened to Georgette. Knowing him, she would probably assume that he would play some part in the investigation.

By half past nine, Ted Beresford was on the telephone.

'Pat, I'm in the dickens of a jam. I ought to go and see Joan—I've managed to wangle a seat on the noon 'plane—and yet—'

'You go and see Joan,' said Dawlish, decidedly. Then added: 'We can manage quite well without you for a few days. Ask Tim to stand by, and tell Felicity that I am behaving myself, won't you?'

Ted chuckled.

'The question is, will she believe me?'

Dawlish cackled obligingly and rang off. It was now a quarter to ten. He would have to hurry in order to reach Marlborough Street in time for the hearing. He did not trouble to fetch his car from a garage in Piccadilly, but took a taxi to the court.

As the cab turned the corner, a surging mass of people filled the pavement and the roadway. Not a tenth of them would be able to enter the court room. Dawlish managed to push his way through until he was within sight of the entrance, which was guarded by a sergeant and two constables.

He caught the sergeant's eye, and called:

'Is Superintendent Trivett there?'

'I think so, sir. You know your way, don't you?'

'Like the palm of my hand,' said Dawlish.

He squeezed his way in, crossed the bleak, stone hall to a small room where Trivett, Munk and another policeman in plainclothes were standing.

'Hal-lo!' exclaimed Trivett. 'I thought you wouldn't be able to keep out of it. What are you after?'

'Watching brief,' Dawlish said. 'I'd rather like to know how the lady behaves in court.'

Trivett looked at him thoughtfully.

'I see,' he said. 'So the dinner-party wasn't just for the pleasure of my company! I wondered at the time. Have we room for Major Dawlish, Inspector?'

Munk said sourly: 'There may be just room right at the

back.' He turned aggressively towards Dawlish. 'You'll have to stand.'

Dawlish nodded good-humouredly.

Caleb Old, the magistrate, glanced round at Dawlish, then bent over a notebook on his desk and wrote briefly, as the clerk called the next case.

The door to the cells was opened. A sergeant came out first, followed by a constable and Georgette. She stepped imperiously into the dock; beautiful, impeccably groomed, entirely composed.

Munk took the oath in a parade ground voice and proceeded to give evidence of identification and arrest. The formal charge followed: *Committing assault upon the person of Nathanial Fairweather with intent to murder.*

'And the police ask for a remand, your worship, pending further inquiries into the case,' added Munk, woodenly.

'I see.' Old turned shrewd eyes towards Georgette. 'Has the accused anything to say?' he asked.

'I did not assault Mr. Fairweather,' Georgette said in a firm, carrying voice.

'You do not appear to be legally represented in court.'

'I am not,' said Georgette, causing a rustle of surprise.

The magistrate turned to Munk.

'You ask for a remand in custody, I presume?'

'Yes, your worship.'

Old hesitated, then shrugged his shoulders.

'Very well. The accused will be remanded in custody for a period of eight days.' He paused. 'Next case, please.'

As he turned to his papers, a door at the back of the court-room burst open, and Richard Lloyd appeared.

CHAPTER SEVEN

THE 'DRUNK' MOTORIST

As Lloyd pushed violently past a constable, Dawlish thought that he was going to make a scene. Georgette, too, for the first time that morning, looked distressed and alarmed.

Every eye was turned towards the newcomer. He made a striking figure and seemed oblivious of everyone but the woman in the dock. The court-room was silent, and no one stirred.

Dawlish made a movement and succeeded in catching Lloyd's attention. He shook his head vigorously as Georgette was helped down from the dock. Next moment she was safely outside.

Lloyd turned and elbowed his way out of the court room, then rushed at Munk who was waiting with Trivett to see Dawlish.

'Why the devil wasn't Miss Lee represented?' he demanded harshly. 'If you—'

'She didn't want a solicitor,' Munk reported as aggressively.

Trivett sent him a warning glance and spoke in a friendly voice.

'Miss Lee had an opportunity to send for her solicitor but refused,' he said, 'and as this was only a formal hearing, her decision has in no way affected the issue. Before she goes to Holloway, would you care to see her for a few minutes?'

Fury gave way to hope.

'Indeed I would!'

'Inspector, go and tell Miss Lee that Mr. Lloyd would like to see her.'

Trivett waited until Munk had gone, before looking from Dawlish to Lloyd and back again.

'You two know each other, I gather.'

'We met a few days ago,' said Dawlish, 'and last night Mr. Lloyd asked me if I would lend a hand in the case.'

'I *see*,' said Trivett. 'I should have known that was why you went to the Carilon Club early this morning, Mr. Lloyd—I saw that in the report of your accident.'

'Accident?' echoed Dawlish, deceitfully.

'Didn't you know?' asked Trivett. 'Mr. Lloyd was involved in a car smash after he'd left you.'

'What happened?'

'The driver was drunk,' said Lloyd, abruptly. 'I—'

He broke off, as Munk came back to say that Georgette would see him.

Dawlish said abruptly: 'What about this accident, Bill? Was it a drunken driver?'

'Yes. He's the next up for hearing,' Trivett said. 'He'd been to a night club and came tearing round the corner—according to a witness, only Lloyd's quick action saved a really nasty smash.'

'Odd,' said Dawlish. 'The smash must have occurred after three a.m.; most night clubs are closed down long before that.'

'Now don't start imagining things, Pat,' laughed Trivett. 'Ah, there he is.'

A small, plumpish man passed into the court room. With a wave of his hand to Trivett Dawlish slipped in after him.

It appeared that his name was Albert Cooper, his profession that of commercial traveller. In a brisk, self-assured voice he admitted that he had been drunk while at the wheel of his car. He was very sorry, he said—he had been celebrating with a friend, and had not realized how much drink he had taken.

It was evident that Caleb Old did not like his manner; the magistrate was brusque and short with him. A constable gave evidence of seeing the car swing round through Admiralty Arch.

'Is this the accused's first offence?' asked Old.

'There is nothing recorded against him, sir,' said a plain-clothes sergeant.

'I see.' Old bent his gaze on the 'drunk' motorist. 'You have admitted that you were guilty of being in charge of a car while under the influence of drink, and as a result of your folly you narrowly escaped causing serious injury to yourself and to another man. You do not appear to be very conscious of your guilt.'

'I've said I'm sorry, sir,' retorted Cooper.

'I see.' Caleb Old looked down at his book. 'Well, we will make doubly sure of it. You will pay fifty pounds and costs and your driving licence will be suspended for twelve months. Next case!'

The sentence seemed to cast Cooper down, all the bounce appeared to leave him; but as he went out Dawlish saw that he was smiling.

Dawlish turned round, and found Trivet just behind him. He was looking at the convicted motorist thoughtfully.

'Very cheerful, isn't he?' murmured Dawlish.

'Yes, considering he nearly committed manslaughter,' Trivett said. They moved into the passage together. 'Now do, for once, listen to me, Pat,' he went on. 'If you're thinking of taking any part in this affair, forget it. It's a dirty business, and not your kind of case at all. There's no doubt whatever that Georgette

Lee is guilty. Fairweather had just settled twenty thousand pounds on her—the capital to go to her on his death. As I see it, Fairweather surprised her at Lloyd's flat. They had a row, and when he turned his back she bashed him. The weapon was an iron ornament taken from the window-sill,' he added, 'and her prints are all over it.'

'All neatly sewn up and waiting only to see whether the old man dies so as to make it a murder charge,' murmured Dawlish. 'Georgette even left a note so that you'd know she'd been there.'

'She would have written that before Fairweather came in,' Trivett reported, 'and after she'd attacked the old boy she forgot it.'

'I wonder why she refused legal aid,' said Dawlish.

'She knows she hasn't a leg to stand on, and she's going to rely on sob stuff,' Trivett said. 'She's a callous piece of work and if I were you I wouldn't waste another minute on her. You might try to convince young Lloyd what a fool he's making of himself—apart from that, forget it.'

'It isn't going to be so easy to forget,' Dawlish told him. 'Oh, Georgette may have attacked the old man—but *why*, William? He had provided her with a good income, and she certainly didn't kill him in order to get the capital. It would be too obvious. I'd go deeper if I were you. For instance, I'd keep a watchful eye on Mr. Cooper.'

'Meaning?'

'That I think he pretended to be drunk and that he may have been trying to kill Lloyd,' said Dawlish. 'And after this, William, you can't say that I've kept anything back! Ah, here's Lloyd. I'm going to take him to lunch.'

Lloyd did not speak on the way to the Carilon, but sat by Dawlish's side staring blankly ahead of him. Not until they were seated at lunch did he pass any comment, then he said bitterly:

'I don't think we can do anything now.'

'We can try,' said Dawlish.

'What's the use of trying if Georgette won't help? I can't understand it, Dawlish, she's changed so much. It's as if something's forcing her to keep silent, almost as if she admitted that she attacked the old man. But I don't believe she did.'

'If you're suggesting that someone's bringing influence to bear on her, I think you're right,' Dawlish said briskly. 'But what really matters is why your uncle was attacked, and why they tried to kill you.' He saw Lloyd start, and followed up his advantage quickly. 'In spite of the evidence that Cooper was drunk, I think he was stone sober. He meant to wreck you. He had a powerful car which would have made a complete wreck of yours and give him a pretty fair chance of escaping uninjured.'

'Nonsense! He was so drunk he could hardly speak!'

'He pretended to be,' Dawlish said. 'Lloyd, you've got to clear your mind of everything else and face up to this: last night attempts were made both on your life and your uncle's.'

'It's impossible!'

'My dear chap, it happened,' Dawlish said. 'The only way you can help Georgette is by finding out the reason for the attacks. Who would profit by two deaths in the family?'

'Profit?'

'Yes—inherit the family fortune,' said Dawlish.

Lloyd said: 'Good Lord! You don't think—look here, Dawlish, you can put that idea right out of your head. I've only two relatives, an aunt and a cousin. They're both comfortably off, and in any case they're the most harmless pair imaginable.' He actually laughed.

'I'd like to know who they are,' Dawlish said stubbornly.

'Well, if you want to waste time, I can't help it,' said Lloyd. 'Aunt Phoebe and Floss wouldn't kill a fly. They've a nice little house in Woking and everything they want.'

'Can I have their address?' Dawlish asked.

'*The Pines,* Guildford Road,' Lloyd told him. He sat on the bed and looked at Dawlish curiously. 'I can't make you out,' he confessed. 'Last night you made a wild guess that Pop was involved in some secret business which might explain the attack, now you're starting another hare.'

Dawlish grinned.

'Not coming up to expectations, eh?'

'Frankly, no.'

Dawlish leaned forward, touching the other's shoulder.

'Last night I wasn't at all sure that there was anything for me to do. Now I'm quite sure that there's plenty to be done. Even the police are, I think, beginning to wonder whether it's all as straight-forward as it seems. What made you late in court, by the way?'

Lloyd looked shame-faced.

'I overslept,' he confessed. 'I didn't get home until nearly five o'clock this morning, and I just lay down in my clothes. The next thing I knew was that it was a quarter to ten! I'd meant to get hold of a solicitor, too. I think if I'd seen Georgette before the hearing I might have persuaded her to act differently, but—'

'Don't try to persuade Georgette about anything,' advised Dawlish, 'just dig into the facts and let me know what you find out. And don't forget to be careful.'

'Do you seriously think that I'm in any danger?'

'So much so that I'm going to ask a friend of mine to keep an eye on you,' Dawlish said. 'You'll like Tim Jeremy, and he's used to odd happenings. Oh—if you hear from your aunt or cousin that I've been to see them, don't be surprised. I shall probably introduce myself as an old friend of yours.'

'I suppose you know what you're doing,' Lloyd said, dejectedly.

He was a little more cheerful after he had met Tim. The two men appeared to like each other on sight. Dawlish left them together and drove to Number 9 Middleton Street.

There was no answer to his ring, but as he moved away, a young man turned briskly into the gate, with an elderly couple beside him.

He stared curiously at Dawlish.

'Have you a permit to view, sir?'

'Is the house for sale?' countered Dawlish.

'Oh, yes, sir. If you will wait just one moment—'

He unlocked the door, and ushered the couple in, inviting them to go wherever they wished. Then, obviously scenting a possible client, he returned to Dawlish.

Ten minutes later Dawlish left him; he now knew the sad story of the house which Fairweather did not buy, and he wondered if Bert's note had helped to change the old man's mind.

Whoever had sent Bert with that note must have learned very quickly that Fairweather contemplated buying.

Musing on this, Dawlish returned to the car and headed for Woking.

The Pines was about half-a-mile out of town, and he found it easily from description that Lloyd had given him. The house was in a charming setting, with rising wooded land beyond it, and sweeping lawn in front. An elderly woman was giving detailed instructions to a man leaning on a rake.

Dawlish drove past, then turned. The gardener was now alone, raking the flower beds with brisk, inexperienced movements. It was these movements, so unlike the slow methodical way of an orthodox gardener, that first caught Dawlish's eye.

He looked again, and as he did so, recognized Bert May.

CHAPTER EIGHT

AUNT AND COUSIN

Bert gaped at Dawlish, who hesitated for a moment before jerking his head forward and driving on; a little way along the road Dawlish turned a corner and pulled up.

Presently the little man came in sight, carrying the rake over his shoulder.

'Lord help us, you don't lose much time!' he grumbled in unwilling admiration. 'I only came out here this afternoon. Told to knock at the door and ask for work, gardening and odd jobs. Gardening!' He sniffed.

'And you were hired on the spot?'

'Like a shot,' said Bert. He was talking quickly and nervously. 'What do you want me for?'

'I want to meet the lady of the house,' said Dawlish. 'Did you have any other orders?'

'None. I was at the *Lion* waiting for a drink when a chap wearing a red ribbon sidled up. Gave me a quid for my fare and told me to come along here. That's all I know about it. You want me to do something?'

'I want to know if any of the people who visited Georgette Lee call here,' said Dawlish.

'Okay.' Bert's eyes shone craftily. 'You calling at the house?' he added.

'Yes, but I don't think I'll be there long. You cut along back before you're missed.'

Dawlish reversed and drove back to *The Pines,* Lloyd's Aunt Phoebe still pottering round the garden gave him a puzzled smile of greeting as he walked across the lawn towards her.

Dawlish said genially: 'I'm so sorry to arrive without warning, Mrs. Fairweather, but your nephew asked me to call as I was coming out this way.'

'You mean *Richard*? Oh then, perhaps you have news of my brother-in-law!' exclaimed Mrs. Fairweather. 'I've been so worried about him. They promised, at the hospital, to telephone me if his condition became worse. It hasn't, has it?'

'No, no change,' said Dawlish.

'Well, that's something,' she said, gratefully. 'It's so nice of you to call—do come in.' She led the way towards the front door, glancing at Bert, who was just entering the garden again. 'These gardeners,' she grumbled, 'I do declare I thought he'd decided to leave, taking my rake with him. I've only just engaged him,' she added. 'Flossie. Flossie! A friend of Richard's has come to see us,' she called.

She led the way into a drawing-room, which, though rather olde worldey, possessed a distinct charm.

'Isn't it lucky?' she went on. 'Usually I have a round of golf in the afternoon but my daughter has hurt her leg, poor child, so I decided against it. I think she must be picking raspberries,' she explained, 'It's so nice to have fruit from the garden, isn't it? *Do* sit down, Mr.—'

'Dawlish,' supplied Dawlish.

'Mr. Dawlish, and make yourself comfortable,' she said. She glanced first at a chair, then doubtfully at him. 'How nice it is to see a really *big* man,' she went on. 'Men are rather small and puny these days, aren't they—' Her voice trailed away as Dawlish sat down very carefully.

'I mustn't stay long,' he said, 'but Richard thought you would be anxious.'

'Indeed yes. We have been worried out of our wits.'

A large, sullen-faced girl appeared in the doorway, who would, Dawlish decided, if dressed less casually, have been quite handsome.

'*Haven't* we, dear?' asked Mrs. Fairweather, a trifle testily.

'Haven't we what?' demanded Flossie.

'Been worried out of our wits,' repeated her mother.

'*You* have,' said Flossie. 'It doesn't matter to me whether the old boy lives or dies.' She limped towards an upright chair, onto which she dropped with obvious relief.

'I'm sure you exaggerate dear,' said Mrs. Fairweather vaguely. 'This is Mr. Dawlish, a friend of Richard's so nice of him to call and tell us the latest news about your poor uncle, isn't it? You entertain Mr. Dawlish, dear, while I pop the kettle on.'

Dawlish smiled at the girl, but her stare of resentment showed no sign of slackening.

'I suppose you're shocked,' she said indifferently.

'Why on earth should I be?' asked Dawlish.

'Because I told the truth about the old man.' She eased a bandage round her ankle. 'Why did Richard send you out here, anyway? He doesn't usually worry much about us.'

Dawlish looked at her narrowly.

'He said you were sure to be worried,' he lied.

'Oh, Mother worries about anything,' remarked Flossie. 'If you want my opinion, Uncle Nathaniel was a silly old fool to have anything to do with that actress, he might have known something unpleasant would happen. Still it's no business of mine. Why didn't Richard—'

A frightened cry from the kitchen cut her words short.

Next moment there was a crash and the sound of breaking china. Both Dawlish and Flossie rushed from the room in time to see Mrs. Fairweather, standing with her mouth agape and her hands raised, staring out of the window towards the pine copse.

'What on earth's the matter?' demanded Flossie sharply.

'It—it—it's that dreadful creature again!' gasped Mrs. Fairweather. 'I saw him near the trees. Oh, Mr. Dawlish!' she cried, turning round. 'Flossie thinks it's all imagination, but I *swear* he's always prowling about the garden.'

'Nonsense,' said Flossie, repressively. 'Every time you hear a footstep there's a burglar about!'

'I tell you I *saw* him,' declared Mrs. Fairweather. 'Look! He's just peeping out from the trees now!'

She pointed a quivering finger towards the copse.

A man was certainly standing there, staring towards the house. Dawlish could see nothing frightening about him, although the direction of his gaze was a little odd.

He said: 'Don't worry, Mrs. Fairweather. If you will allow me, I'll go and see what the fellow's about.'

Before either of them could speak, he was out of the back door and hurrying towards the end of the garden. He vaulted the fence and strode up the rising grassland towards the copse.

When Dawlish was within fifty yards of the man he turned suddenly and disappeared among the trees.

His movements were swift and easy, and he was quickly lost to sight.

Dawlish quickened his pace.

The copse was not large, and when Dawlish judged that he had reached the middle he turned and looked in all directions. Through gaps in the foliage he could see the back of *The Pines*, but there was no sign of his quarry.

The slender tree trunks were not large enough to hide the man, but he might be lurking in the shadows, crouching among the ferns.

Beyond the copse Dawlish could see the sun shining, but this was an eerie spot.

He felt that he was being watched.

Although he could see no one, he was quite sure that the man had him in view. A gust of wind blew through the trees with a sighing sound.

Dawlish glanced over his shoulder again, but by now *The Pines* was hidden from sight, and he seemed to be cut off from the outside world. He could understand well enough Mrs. Fairweather's nervousness.

Where *was* the fellow?

Of course—his quarry was almost certainly hidden in the boughs of a tree. Branches stuck out, twisted and strong; a dozen men could be within a few yards of Dawlish without his noticing them unless he happened to glance upwards.

But he saw no one, though he imagined that some of the nearer branches were swaying.

He was only a short distance from the far side of the copse, when he heard a sound behind him. He swung round—but no one was in sight. Something rolled close to his feet—a large pine cone. It might have dropped by accident, loosened by the wind; or it might have been thrown at him.

A burst of laughter startled him; it came from the middle of the copse.

Another followed, this time from his right. He turned that way. It seemed plain enough that the man was trying to shake his nerve; he was equally determined that the fellow should not succeed.

But—were there two men? Or was there only one?

Dawlish peered through the trees. Creaking noises seemed to be all about him, and another gust of wind made the pines rustle and groan. He wished he were in the open meadowland beyond, yet was determined not to let anyone drive him away. They were trying to scare him, and—

A pine cone struck him on the shoulder.

It came from the left, and he turned in that direction swiftly. He could see ferns moving, probably where the thrower had been standing. He passed through a little clump of trees, and fancied that he caught a glimpse of a man's head.

Got him! he thought, and brushed some ferns aside.

He heard a rustle above him; there was no doubt about it this time. As he glanced up, he saw a man's legs dangling above his head. Next moment the man had dropped on to his shoulders, throwing him forward with the unexpected weight.

Pain shot through him, excruciating, agonizing. Another blow hit the back of his head, and seemed to lift it from his shoulders. He was vaguely conscious of fingers clutching his throat, constricting, pressing, He could not breathe. He strained his great body without any effect; the fingers were like steel. He felt blackness enveloping him; there was a buzzing sound in his ears. All light faded, and he lost consciousness.

CHAPTER NINE

ALARM AMONG FRIENDS

In his London flat, that afternoon, Richard Lloyd told Tim that he found it difficult to think of anything but Georgette, in spite of the distractions Dawlish had created. It would have been easier had he seen any purpose in Dawlish's suggestions, but he could see none. Georgette's manner when he had seen her at Marlborough Street filled him with dismay, he said—she had been so determined not to accept help, so fatalistic and so appealingly beautiful.

Dawlish's plan to visit Woking was another crazy notion: Dawlish seemed to be much over-rated, and while Lloyd admitted that he was glad to have Tim at hand, he protested that Tim did not take the affair seriously enough.

Tim eyed Lloyd sleepily.

'Have some beer—it always helps me to think.'

Lloyd jumped up.

'What's the use of sitting here drinking all the afternoon!' he cried passionately. 'I thought Dawlish would do something more constructive than saddle me with a drinking companion!'

Tim blinked.

'Well, what good are you doing?' demanded Lloyd. 'If you

think you're protecting me you're mistaken—I can look after myself. What's more, I don't think Dawlish knows what he's talking about. *I'm* in no danger!'

Tim looked at him in mild disapproval.

'I can't agree to that,' he said. 'Pat wouldn't say you were if you weren't. Believe me, when he sees the red light it's there whether you can see it or not. Matter of fact,' he went on, in his deep, rather sleepy voice, 'he didn't ask me to follow you around because he thought someone might bump you off—there isn't much I can do if anyone tries,' he added philosophically. 'Sorry, but there it is. One shot out of a passing car, one shove under a nasty bus, one grain of poison in the old coffee, and you'd be turning your toes up. No, Pat sent me to make sure *you* don't do anything silly.'

Lloyd glared.

'If you're trying to make me lose my temper—'

'Oh, my dear chap! A thousand times no. You've practically done that for yourself, haven't you? Now be a good lad and pour me out another—'

He broke off as the telephone bell rang.

Lloyd snatched up the receiver while Tim eyed him speculatively, noting the signs of overwrought nerves. This wasn't a condition due only to the recent happenings. Had Lloyd a secret trouble, Tim wondered.

Lloyd was speaking over the telephone in a taut, highly-strung voice.

'Yes, this *is* Richard Lloyd . . . Who . . . Who? I can't—oh, Aunt Phoebe. What . . . *What?* . . . Er, yes,' he went on in a startled voice, looking round at Tim, 'yes, I asked him to call . . . That's odd, isn't it? How long ago?'

Tim uncoiled himself from his chair and moved towards the telephone.

'I see,' said Lloyd at last. 'No, I can't understand it. I'll ring you back, Aunt Phoebe, good-bye.' He replaced the receiver slowly.

'Well?' Tim asked.

'What trick's Dawlish up to now?' demanded Lloyd, his voice still harsh. 'My aunt says he called there about half past three, went off to look for a man who was hiding in the copse near the house, and didn't come back. My cousin and the gardener went to look for him, but found no trace. It's half past five now,' he added with a glance at the clock. 'She said his car's still parked outside the house.'

Tim laid a hand on his shoulder.

'Now listen to me,' he said. 'Pat does some mysterious things and it isn't always easy to guess what he's up to, but he wouldn't dodge off for the sake of being mysterious. Feel like a drive?'

'You mean—'

'I mean I'd like to go to Woking,' said Tim. 'May I use the telephone?' He had the instrument in his hand as he spoke and dialled a number. Lloyd saw the changed expression on his face. Tim Jeremy was serious at last.

'I want to speak to Mr. Derek Gillow, please . . . Yes, I'll hold on.' He put his hand over the mouthpiece. 'Friend of Pat's,' he told Lloyd briefly. 'Hallo, Derek? . . . Tim here . . . Trouble . . . Pat may have gone off on one of his solo flights but I don't think it's likely. He expected to be back early this evening . . . Ten minutes, old boy . . . That's fine.' He replaced the receiver and cocked an eyebrow at Lloyd. 'Coming?'

'Is there really any point in—'

'Please yourself,' Tim said. 'I'm going.'

Seven minutes later, with Lloyd sitting beside him, he pulled up his Talbot outside a house in Jermyn Street. A Lagonda was parked against the kerb, and the man at the wheel waved to Tim as he got out.

Gillow, a broad-shouldered chunky man with a brick-red face and hard, frosty eyes was introduced to Lloyd, and in a matter of seconds the two cars, one a hundred yards in front of the other, were heading for Woking.

A little rambling and *distrait,* Aunt Phoebe told her story to the three men. Flossie confirmed it, and a shabby little man still working in the garden agreed that he had actually spoken to Dawlish. He went further, adding that though he had found no one in the copse, he had heard someone laugh.

'Fair gave me the creeps,' he added.

'And it's so peculiar,' said Aunt Phoebe. 'We had a cup of tea all ready for him, I actually poured it out, thinking he would be back any minute, and he just didn't come. What *do* you think we ought to do?'

'Have a look at the copse,' said Tim, promptly.

'You'd be wasting your time,' said Flossie, morosely. 'We've looked.'

Tim regarded her thoughtfully.

'No two people see the same thing in the same way,' he told her sunnily, 'and quite a few don't even see the same thing.'

Flossie scowled.

'We'll be back soon Mrs. Lloyd and I shouldn't worry too much. Mr. Dawlish is quite capable of looking after himself.'

An hour later, Tim was much more troubled, for the three men had found unmistakable signs of a struggle.

Lloyd drove Tim's car back. Derek drove his own and Tim took Dawlish's Bentley. He parted company with the others in Victoria Street, and went straight to Trivett's top floor flat.

Trivett himself opened the door. On seeing Tim he gave a dramatic groan.

'*Now* what are you after? I suppose you'd better come in.'

'I'm worried about Pat,' Tim announced abruptly.

'I'm always worried about Pat,' said Trivett, drily. 'Sit down, Tim.'

'He's missing,' announced Tim. 'I'm serious.' He looked sombre in the good light. 'It may be a mare's nest, but . . .'

Trivett listened without interruption as he explained what had happened.

'I don't know that there's much you can do, Bill,' he finished, 'except put out a call. I'm pretty certain Pat walked into trouble in that copse. You can worry about the implications of it later. Just now, our job is to find him.'

Trivett rubbed his chin.

'Yes,' he agreed. 'I'll speak to the Woking police and ask them to make inquiries. Mind you,' he added as he went to the telephone, 'I'm not a bit sure that you need be alarmed. Pat's always managed to look after himself.'

'That's why I'm worried,' Tim said. 'This time he hasn't.'

Trivett dialled a number.

'Just what is he up to?' he asked.

'Helping Lloyd,' said Tim. 'He thinks Lloyd's in danger—it looks as if he thinks the rest of the family might be in the same boat. But he didn't say very much to me. He simply asked me to keep an eye on Lloyd.'

But there was no news of Dawlish that day, and no report of any kind came in.

Next morning Trivett himself went to Woking, and talked to Aunt Phoebe and Flossie. Flossie said bluntly that she thought a lot of fuss was being made about nothing; Mrs. Fairweather on the other hand was in a state of great agitation. At one time she had always been quite happy to walk across the fields to the golf course, but ever since she had seen *that* man about, she had been nervous, and refused to take the short cut on her own. She was sure that he prowled round the house every night; she was always hearing strange noises in the garden.

Flossie looked contemptuous when Trivett promised to have *The Pines* watched by the police.

No lurking prowler put in an appearance that day, however; nor did Dawlish.

Grace Trivett was a brave and patient woman, resigned to the inevitability of her husband being called out at all hours of the night. She was alone that evening, when the front door bell rang.

Opening the door she saw her caller to be Felicity Dawlish, tense, white-faced.

'Grace, is Bill here?'

'Why, Felicity! Come in. No,' she added, 'Bill's gone out on a case. My dear, you look worried!' She led the way into the living-room.

'I *am* worried!' exclaimed Felicity. 'I can't find Pat and I can't find Tim. They say at the club that Pat wasn't there last night, but his car's in the garage—they told me Tim garaged it the day before yesterday.' She stood staring at Trivett's wife. 'Grace, is anything the matter?'

'Well, my dear, you know what Pat is,' said Grace, 'whenever anything happens that attracts his attention he's off like a shot—I don't think there's any need for all this fuss.'

'Fuss!' echoed Felicity. 'Then—'

'I don't know very much about it, but I can tell you a little. Would you like a cup of tea?' When Felicity did not respond, Grace said comfortably: 'Let's go into the kitchen, I can make a cup of tea while I'm talking.'

Felicity followed her, listening intently.

The kettle began to boil as Grace finished.

'And I think Pat will find his way out of any difficulty,' she said. 'He always has in the past, my dear, and habits stick. I thought you were in Paris,' she added.

'There was a vacant seat on the evening 'plane, and I gathered from Ted Beresford that Pat was up to something,' Felicity explained. 'Grace—*is* Bill worried?'

Grace poured the boiling water into the teapot.

'He is a little,' she said, 'but then it's his job to be. Hand me that tray off the shelf, will you, and we'll take the tea into the other room. It wouldn't surprise me if Pat were to reappear any moment,' she went on. 'Now sit down and take off your coat.'

Dawlish did not turn up that night.

It was nearly twelve o'clock when Trivett returned home, bringing Tim Jeremy with him. They did not attempt to hide their alarm from Felicity, who, at Grace's insistence, was staying for the night.

She was lying stonily staring into the darkness when the telephone bell rang. At once she flung the bedclothes back and jumped out of bed. She heard Trivett's voice, sharp and questioning, and then an exclamation of surprised relief: 'Why, *Pat*!'

Felicity rushed into the next room.

CHAPTER TEN

ORDEAL FOR DAWLISH

Trivett was sitting up in bed, holding the telephone, when Felicity rushed into the room. '*Shh!*' enjoined Grace, and Felicity nodded and stood quite still, watching Trivett, who was listening intently.

Grace whispered: 'You'll catch cold, Felicity.' She lifted a wrap. 'Put this round your shoulders—'

'*Quiet!*' hissed Trivett. 'Pat, speak louder, I can't hear you. Pat—'

He stopped abruptly.

Felicity took a step towards him.

'Pat, speak *louder,*' urged Trivett. 'Pat!'

There was a deathly silence in the room.

After an interminable pause, Trivett began to tap the telephone rest up and down, recalling the exchange. There was a long wait before he spoke.

'I am Superintendent Trivett of Scotland Yard, operator, and I want you to trace that call . . . Yes, I'll speak to the supervisor.' He paused, looking at Felicity. 'Pat says that he's all right,' he reassured her, 'but he doesn't know where he is—he's being kept prisoner. He wants us to locate the house but not try to rescue him yet, he thinks he can learn a lot by staying put.'

'Oh, Pat!' exclaimed Felicity, tears of relief, of exasperation, choking her voice.

Trivett smiled grimly.

'He seems confident enough, I shouldn't worry too much. He also urges us to watch Fairweather and young Lloyd very closely—I—hallo, Supervisor, I am . . .'

Dawlish replaced the receiver gently. The faint ting! of the bell sounded loud in the dark, quiet hall. He looked anxiously towards the landing. A diffused light came from a room upstairs and he imagined he could hear the murmur of voices. There were shadows on the landing, dark vague shapes—possibly the shadows of men. He did not know whether he was being watched, he did not even know whether he had been overheard.

The front door, he had already discovered, was locked and bolted. Outside, he knew that a guard was on duty. But there would be an even chance of escape in the darkness; all that he needed to do was turn the key and draw back the bolts.

He had just told Trivett that he thought he could do more good by staying here. Now, the temptation to break out was almost overpowering.

He turned away abruptly, approaching the stairs, peering upwards to see if the shadows were caused by crouching men. This was a strange, uncanny household—a house where silence reigned, nerve-racking, endless.

He was not thinking of the past two days as he mounted the stairs; but they had not been good days.

He reached the first landing and waited again. The banister-rail was cold to his touch, and there was a clammy atmosphere about the house, as if it had not been lived-in for a long time.

He reached the second landing.

The light was coming from the next floor; a door was ajar and one streak of bright light lay like a spear. His own room was on this landing, and the door was closed. Dawlish crept slowly towards it. Now that he was free, would he be wise to look into the other rooms and try to learn more about the layout of the house, or would that be tempting providence too far?

He had been locked in . . .

His thoughts went back to the moment when he had woken up and found himself in that room. His head had ached badly and his neck had been stiff, and for a while he had not remembered what had happened. Then he had recalled the incidents in the copse, and had become wide awake, sitting up and looking about him.

He remembered making a great effort to get out of bed, stumbling noisily. The door had been opened, not briskly or furiously, but with a slow, intimidating precision. Two men had come in, powerful fellows who had not uttered a word.

Dawlish touched his chin.

It was swollen and painful from the blows which had been rained upon him then. His assailants had left him half-conscious, and he had been left alone for many hours, his only food and drink, water and a small piece of bread.

That the men who held him captive wanted to break his spirit, hoping that he would talk freely, was obvious enough. It was not going to be easy to withstand them. His tormentors were skilful and persistent, and the atmosphere of mystery and brooding menace assisted them.

He had spoken very little.

A man had wakened him the previous night, standing by the bedside, faintly visible through the shadows. The questions had come relentlessly. Chiefly, they had to do with Nathaniel Fairweather—some vague, and undoubtedly misleading, but they had helped to convince him that there was much more in this affair than the hysterical rage of a woman who had been thrown aside.

No one had yet visited him tonight and he had spent over an hour at the door, picking the lock with a piece of metal.

His knife and everything which might be used as a skeleton key had been taken away from him, but his jailors had forgotten the chains by which the electric shade was suspended. He had taken the shade down, removed a link from each of three chains, then put everything back in position. Next, he had hidden two of the links beneath the carpet, and worked on the third with coins. He had managed to straighten it until it could be pushed into the lock, but it was really too thick for such delicate work. The task had been laborious; time and time again he had felt like giving up; even now he remembered the thrill of satisfaction when the lock had clicked back.

He had waited, in case the sound had been heard.

Leaving the room and going down the stairs had been nerve-racking, finding the telephone in a corner of the hall a triumph.

Well, he had got through to Trivett and now the question was: *should* he look into the other rooms? The more he knew about the house the better it would be later, when the moment arrived for him to escape.

He decided to take no further risks that night, and went to his own room.

Tired now that the stimulus of effort had gone, he found the light switch and pressed it down, narrowing his eyes against the sudden light.

A man's voice said: 'Where have you been, Dawlish?'

Dawlish stood quite still; only his eyes moved. The speaker, he saw, was young and sharp-featured. There was a gun in his hand.

'Where have you been?' he demanded.

Dawlish relaxed a little and moved forward.

'Just finding my way about,' he said.

'What did you do?'

'I walked down the stairs and walked up again,' answered Dawlish.

'How did you unlock the door?'

Dawlish looked puzzled.

'Door? Oh, *this* door! My dear chap, why didn't you say so?'

'This is no time for being funny,' said the thin-faced man, in his harsh, monotonous way. 'What tool did you use?'

Dawlish glanced up at the light. The room would be searched for his tool, obstinacy over this would get him nowhere.

'If you've an eye for distance you'll see that the lamp's a shade higher than it was,' he said. He took out the little tool and tossed it on to the bed. 'The other links are under the carpet near the wardrobe. The secret's out—next, please.'

'Whom did you telephone?'

This question almost caught Dawlish unawares; could they have listened-in to the conversation? It was impossible to be sure how much this man knew.

'I think I've said enough,' decided Dawlish.

The man moved slowly towards him. Dawlish leaned back. If there were any threat of violence, he would use his feet—he did not intend to let them knock him about again. The other stopped a couple of yards away from him, with the gun pointing towards Dawlish's stomach.

He said slowly: 'We didn't bring you here for fun, Dawlish.'

'I'm quite prepared to believe that,' Dawlish said languidly.

'And if you don't do what we want, you'll be killed.'

Dawlish snapped his fingers.

'Just like that?' he asked.

'Just like that,' agreed the other gravely.

'Obviously I've become mixed up with the wrong kind of people,' Dawlish said, sunnily.

He smiled into the man's face, and his expression gave no inkling of the thoughts running through his head. If he slid forward, swinging his legs round at the same time, he might be able to catch the man unawares. It would be comforting to have the gun instead of being threatened with it.

Dawlish moved.

He put all the strength he could into the swing of his legs, catching the other just below the knee. The surprise was complete, the man staggered sideways and his arms waved. Dawlish sprang to his feet, and snatched the gun.

'Now we can talk,' he said gently.

The other shot a quick glance towards the door.

'I don't think I'd bring the others along just yet, if I were you,' Dawlish said. 'There could be repercussions.'

'Dawlish, I warn you—'

'*Hush!*' counselled Dawlish. 'You're the one in danger now. I've got the gun. Remember? May I have your coat?'

The other hesitated.

'Toss it over to me,' said Dawlish, his voice sharpening.

The man stripped sullenly and threw the coat to Dawlish. Still holding the gun in position Dawlish caught it, felt for the inside pocket, and drew out a wallet.

'Turn round and face the wall,' he ordered. He waited until the man had obeyed, then looked at the black leather wallet, which was crammed with papers. There was a lot of money in one pound and five pound notes, and three letters. Each was addressed:

Aubrey Wilmot, Esq., 11, Merridale Street, Wembley, Middlesex.

'All right as far as it goes, Aubrey—may I call you Aubrey?'

said Dawlish pleasantly. 'The point is, I'm hungry. Is anyone guarding the kitchen?'

Wilmot shook his head.

'Good!' Dawlish opened the door and glanced rapidly up and down the deserted passage. He knew that he was taking a risk, but the lure of food was overwhelming. 'Now you lead me to the kitchen, and if you take a false step you won't know what's hit you. Don't hurry,' he added, 'and don't make any noise.'

He followed Wilmot closely. One square meal would certainly make a world of difference. Sullenly Wilmot led the way into a large, old-fashioned kitchen with a stone floor. Dawlish glanced at the clock on the mantelpiece; it was a quarter to three.

'Food, Aubrey,' he ordered.

Wilmot sent him a malevolent glance, but obeyed. He took the remains of a meat pie out of the refrigerator, together with some butter and a loaf of bread.

Within two minutes, Dawlish was sitting down to the meal and the gas was hissing under a kettle in the scullery.

'That's much better,' he said. 'Do you know how to make tea?'

With hands which trembled Wilmot put three teaspoonfuls of tea into the pot, and picked up the kettle.

Next moment, he flung it at Dawlish!

CHAPTER ELEVEN

BOILING WATER

A stream of boiling water spurted from the spout and missed Dawlish's face by inches. The kettle sailed past his head, a trail of drips falling on his head and shoulders before crashing to the stone floor. Dawlish staggered back as Wilmot leapt at him, striking at the hand which held the gun.

Dawlish struck out blindly, and caught him a swinging blow on the side of the head, but it needed more than that to stop Wilmot, who clawed the gun away and then struck at Dawlish's face.

The gun was now in Wilmot's hand, and he raised it, in two minds whether to strike with the butt, or shoot.

'I've had it,' thought Dawlish.

'*Wilmot!*'

The name cut through the man's passion like a knife. Wilmot lowered the gun in automatic obedience.

Dawlish leaned against the sink, too spent to give more than a cursory glance to the man standing in the doorway.

He was wearing a heavy overcoat, the collar turned up, as if he wanted to avoid recognition. Curtly he ordered Wilmot from the room.

Wilmot caught his breath, hesitated, then slunk towards the door. For the first time Dawlish saw that his saviour was not alone; a tall, thin man, careless of being recognized, moved from behind him. He looked not unsympathetically at Dawlish's scratched and blistered face.

'What's the trouble?'

'Scalds, and a scratch,' Dawlish said.

The man in the overcoat looked at him.

'We will have them dressed,' he promised. 'I didn't intend anything like this, Dawlish. I'm sorry.'

'I assure you that I didn't intend it either,' murmured Dawlish.

The tall, thin man, signing to Dawlish to follow, took him first to a bathroom where he attended with some care to his injuries, and then back to his bedroom.

'If you were a reasonable human being you'd have stayed in bed,' he said. 'Are you all right now?'

'Quite, except that I was really looking forward to a cup of tea.'

The other chuckled.

'I'll see you get one,' he promised. 'Don't stroll out of the room, though, we might think you were trying to escape. Ah, here's the great man.'

He came into the room, no longer wearing his coat. He had broad, unusual features, and his eyes narrowed unnaturally. When he spoke, his voice was deep and mellow and Dawlish decided it was the only really genuine thing about him, and that he was cleverly, and heavily, disguised.

'All right, Max,' the newcomer said to the tall man, 'get that tea—is there anything else you want, Dawlish?'

'Not until I've had some sleep,' Dawlish said.

'You won't be disturbed,' promised the other, soothingly.

'You *are* trying to make me feel at home,' said Dawlish with a chuckle. 'What's it all about?'

'It's too long a story to be told tonight,' said the other, 'but, in fact, I want your help—and I can't say how angry I am that you have been treated so badly. I'd like to say this. I think you and I have much in common. We are equally anxious to contribute to the public good. Our methods are somewhat different but when I tell you what I want to do, I think you will agree that I'm not unreasonable. If we can't come to an agreement—' He broke off and shrugged his shoulders. 'Well, I hope we'll part on good terms. Ask for anything you want, won't you?'

'Oh, I certainly will,' said Dawlish.

'Good! Good night.'

'Good night,' echoed Dawlish, faintly.

Daylight filled the room when Dawlish woke up. Gradually the events of the night came to his mind. Those unnaturally broad features—what *was* the explanation of them?

Paraffin wax, injected under the skin, could broaden a man's features and completely alter his appearance for some weeks. Plastic surgery would make an even better job. Whatever the secret, Dawlish felt convinced that the man was disguised.

'Max', on the other hand, was his natural self.

Dawlish remembered the tall, lanky figure, the humorous mouth and the gleam in the brown eyes. Yes, he liked Max. But their combined efforts to reassure him and to win his sympathy was puzzling—it certainly did not square with Wilmot's attitude, and it was difficult to believe that Wilmot had not acted on instructions. It seemed more likely that 'the Boss' had changed his mind; yet Max was certainly a different type from Wilmot, and *seemed* sincere.

Suddenly Dawlish remembered the letters which he had taken from Wilmot's coat. The wallet had been left on the bed, but he had put the letters in his pocket. He stretched out an arm for his coat, which was hanging on the back of a chair, and slipped his fingers into the pocket. He found what he wanted.

He took the letters out and pushed them beneath the bedclothes, feeling suddenly afraid that he might be watched. A quick glance round the room, however, removed his fears. The ceiling and the walls above the picture rail were darkened with ingrained dust, and there were certainly no slits through which he could be spied on.

The door opened quietly.

Immediately alert to danger, Dawlish pushed the letters more firmly out of sight. But it was only Max carrying a tray of tea, as genial as he had been the night before. There was a copy of the *Daily Gazette* neatly folded beside the cup.

'I'll leave you to pour out,' he said, 'I can see that you are rested, but no one is rested enough to chat in the early morning.'

As the door closed behind him Dawlish opened the newspaper. Then, as he had half-expected, he saw the headline: *No News Of Major Dawlish.*

'Oh, confound it!' he exclaimed aloud.

Soon he was reading the story . . .

The thing which most worried him was a report that Mrs. Dawlish had returned from Paris the night before. The rest was not really new. There was a rehash of the attack on Fairweather, a picture of Georgette Lee, and a brief résumé of the visit to Woking. So that story had leaked out quickly.

He sipped his tea, frowning in concentration.

He did not think that Trivett would have released the story;

he was quite sure that Tim would not have said a word to the newspapers. The leakage might be from Richard Lloyd or, more likely, one of two women. He found himself thinking a great deal about the surly Flossie.

He read Wilmot's letters next.

Two were from women, couched in much the same terms. The third was an unsigned typewritten note, and gave Dawlish much to think about, for it read:

Your next report will be at Woking.
Leave it in the usual place.

He poured himself out another cup of tea and pondered over the note. Max or 'the Boss' might have sent it. He tucked it away in his coat, leaving the other letters on the floor.

He heard a car speeding away on the gravel outside. A few minutes afterwards another car followed it.

Dawlish frowned, then slipped out on to the landing.

The bathroom door was standing open. On the floor was a jug of steaming water and on a shelf above the hand-basin were a safety razor, soap and brush.

He shaved gingerly, for his face was still tender. He was prepared for another visit from Max, but no one appeared and the house was silent.

He dressed hurriedly.

No attempt was being made to keep him under observation, as far as he could see, and none of the doors on the landing were completely shut. He peered into one of the rooms. The bed was unmade and two drawers in the dressing-table were half-open.

'Hallo!' he exclaimed.

He hurried from room to room, then up to the attic floor,

without seeing a soul. He could hardly believe that the men had gone, and with rising astonishment and some concern he raced downstairs.

The house was empty.

CHAPTER TWELVE

SHOCK FOR TIM

Tim Jeremy parked his car outside his flat in Alyth Mews, and as he did so a duster appeared through the open window and was shaken with extreme vigour.

'Well, well,' mused Tim.

He opened the front door cautiously. The three doors inside were standing open and in the front room someone was not only moving about, but doing so with what Tim uneasily categorized as righteous, and quite unnecessary, energy.

'Oi!' he cried aloud.

Nothing but thumps answering him he ventured another yard or two, thereby catching sight of a flowered overall.

'Felicity! What on earth—'

'Tim,' said Felicity, emerging with a bottle in each hand, 'why didn't you *tell* me you were in a mess like this?'

'Mess? What mess? Go easy, Fel, there may be a drop of beer left in those bottles.'

'Go *easy*! If I had my way I'd get two women in this afternoon and we'd clean the flat from top to bottom. The larder—have you *seen* the larder?'

'The light isn't too good in there,' mumbled Tim. He sidled over to a cupboard and peered inside. 'Gin and something—and a spot of beer.' He poured out the drinks, hopefully, as Felicity sank back on a newly-punched cushion. 'Here's luck,' he said.

There was silence for a moment, and then Felicity said with studied nonchalance:

'There's no news, I suppose?'

'Nothing yet, old girl,' said Tim quietly. 'I've seen Trivett this morning. No definite information has come through. Things are complicated because Pat doesn't want to be rescued yet. So no news is good news.'

'I wish I could think so,' said Felicity.

She was in a different mood now. Her nervous energy had spent itself and worry over her husband had come crowding back. She pushed the scarf back on her head, and blew a wisp of hair out of her eyes.

'Well, the man must be fed. Are we going out to lunch or shall we have a snack here?'

'We are going out,' said Tim, firmly.

Felicity moved restlessly.

'I suppose there isn't anything we can *do*?'

'I don't know of anything,' said Tim, soberly. 'I've been out and about with Derek this morning, and looked in at the Yard. Young Lloyd's still moping and nothing seems to be happening at all. If I could think of anything I'd be after it like a shot—' He broke off, and shrugged.

'I knew Pat would overstep the mark one day,' said Felicity, glumly. 'Oh, well, I suppose I'd better go and tidy up.'

Tim's worried gaze followed her as she went out. Although he had pretended that he was not really alarmed, he was in fact more worried than he had ever been for his friend. Even

Trivett was not at all happy about the complete silence which had followed Pat's one telephone call.

Tim lit a cigarette, half-smoked it, and then put out his hand to pick up his glass. He could not find it. He glanced round—

The glass of beer had gone!

He gaped at the table.

No one had been in the room since he had touched the glass, and now—

He swung round, for there was a movement at the window. A hand appeared, holding the empty glass, and Tim's heart thumped against his ribs.

The glass was put on the table and cautiously pushed towards him.

Only when he had recovered from the first shock did Tim recognize the hand. It was large, with long, broad fingers; a very familiar hand.

'Pat, you beggar!' he cried.

The hand stopped moving; next moment Dawlish's face appeared at the window.

'I'm thirsty, too,' remarked Dawlish. 'I hope that isn't the last bottle.'

'You—hound!'

'Oh, come.' Dawlish began to climb in. He had almost reached the floor when the door burst open.

'*Pat!*' cried Felicity.

'Hal-*lo!*' boomed Dawlish. 'So Paris lost its attractions!'

She ran across the room and flung her arms round his neck, tears running down her cheeks.

'Now, steady,' murmured Dawlish, his face in her hair.

At last, Felicity took her arms away and looked closely into Dawlish's eyes.

'All sound in wind and limb,' reported Dawlish, 'with one or two superficial blemishes that won't take long to heal. I'm so sorry, darling. I didn't know what I was walking into, or I would have been more careful.'

'Pat,' implored Felicity, 'don't do that again—don't ever do that again. I know it's useless to say so, and of course I won't try to stop you, but—*please* don't go off without letting me know. I can't, I can't, *bear* it. Pat, your face!'

'Nothing at all to worry about,' Dawlish assured her. 'What about lunch?'

'Felicity has been turning everything upside down and I can't find a blessed thing!' explained Tim plaintively. 'But in spite of some quite uncalled for rudery about the larder, I have two whole tins of corned beef, if only I can lay hands on them! I don't know whether there's enough bread,' he added, 'but I can slip out to gather up some odds and ends. *After* I've been told what all the fun and games are about,' he added firmly.

Dawlish grinned.

'It isn't very complicated,' he declared. 'I was first kidnapped, and then quite unaccountably set free. I think they got the wind up. The sickening thing is that I learned very little about the mystery,' Dawlish went on. 'I haven't even a good story for Bill Trivett. How is he, by the way?'

'Doesn't he know you're back?' asked Felicity.

'No, I came here first,' said Dawlish, simply. 'I fancy that Bill put the police on to the house and when the Boss discovered it he cleared off. I was left high and dry, walked to the nearest main road, caught a bus and was at Walton-on-Thames just in time to catch a train to town. Simple, isn't it?'

'Too simple. I want details,' ordered Tim firmly.

'I'd better give Bill a ring and ask him to come round—you go and do the shopping, and I'll tell the story once for everybody's benefit. Nothing else has happened, I take it?' he added.

'The whole world stopped on its orbit when you disappeared!' cried Tim, dramatically thumping his chest. 'All right, I'll get some delicacies! But only on condition that Felicity doesn't do any more spring cleaning while I'm out,' he added, decidedly.

Felicity made a face at him, and Dawlish went to the telephone.

Over the cold lunch Trivett both listened and expounded.

Dawlish's telephone call had been traced after some difficulty, and it had not been until nearly nine o'clock that morning that the police had moved in towards the house in a lonely spot near Walton. The two car-loads of men had been observed, but there had been too few police to stop them.

'I suppose the car numbers were taken,' Dawlish said.

'Oh, yes,' Trivett assured him, 'but they can change the number plate easily enough. We may pick them up, but I'm not very hopeful. The cars were Packards—'

'Evidence of money. What's the position generally?' asked Dawlish.

Trivett shrugged his shoulders.

'It hasn't really altered,' he said. 'Lloyd's stayed at his flat—possibly because Tim or Gillow have been with him most of the time. Georgette won't say anything and still refuses to call in legal aid—I can't understand her at all. Fairweather will probably recover, by the way.'

'That's one good thing,' remarked Dawlish.

'Apart from that, nothing's turned up,' said Trivett, gloomily. 'If it hadn't been for what happened to you, I just wouldn't believe that this was anything but a straightforward case. Even now—'

'That's right, say that I've been making it up,' said Dawlish.

'Don't be an ass! But every other trail peters out, you know. Even at Woking—'

'Ah,' said Dawlish.

'The fellow who was hiding in the copse had been seen by several people,' said Trivett. 'He was believed to come from a gypsy encampment not far away. But the Romanies say that they know no such man. They could be right, and he was only using them as a cover to watch *The Pines*.'

'Question, why watch *The Pines*?' murmured Dawlish.

'That's what I keep asking myself,' said Trivett. 'There's one little thing, although I haven't done anything about it yet Mrs. Fairweather employed a new gardener—a fellow named May who usually haunts the East End and sleeps in a doss-house—you saw him, didn't you?'

Dawlish nodded.

'He stayed until yesterday and then slipped away after dark. It's odd that he should have turned up at the house just then, isn't it?'

'Give a dog a bad name,' murmured Dawlish.

'It's rarely given in the first place unless it's justified,' said Trivett smugly. 'By the way, young Lloyd said something about you suggesting that the two women at *The Pines* might be behind it.'

'Well, they're certainly connected, since presumably they will inherit something from Fairweather. By the way, can Pop talk yet?'

'He's conscious, but the doctors won't let us question him. The only interesting point is that he's asked for you several times.'

'And you've been holding *that*!' cried Dawlish. He turned to Felicity. 'Good-bye for the moment, my cherub! I'm going sick-visiting!'

CHAPTER THIRTEEN

REQUEST FROM 'POP'

Pop Fairweather lay in bed, his head swathed in bandages. He raised his hand slightly as Dawlish entered.

Dawlish nodded to the nurse, who rose from her seat and left the room, leaving the door ajar.

'Why didn't you come before?' Pop muttered feverishly.

'They wouldn't let me,' said Dawlish.

'Didn't think—you took any notice. My nephew been to see you?'

'Yes.'

'Helping him?'

'Why, yes. He doesn't think Georgette attacked you and I—'

'Georgette? What has she to do with it?'

Dawlish said slowly: 'She was at the flat a little while before you, and the police thought—'

'Damned fools!' declared Pop with the ghost of a snort. 'She'd been and gone when I was attacked.'

Dawlish weighed this startling information in his mind as he regarded the old man.

'Are you sure, Pop?'

'Of course I'm sure. A man hit me—saw the fellow.'

'Would you recognize him?' asked Dawlish.

'I might. Richard's in danger—as well as I. I suppose you realized that.'

'Yes.'

'Look after him,' urged Pop. 'Nice lad, although a bit dull. See that nothing happens to him, Dawlish.'

'I will,' promised Dawlish.

'Good! Now—what have you been doing?'

'Trying to find out what you've been doing,' said Dawlish.

A gleam sprang into the bloodshot eyes, tinged with sardonic amusement.

'Man like myself—prominent—successful—bound to make enemies. I've made plenty. Now someone's hitting back. No idea who. I think—Georgette Lee—'

He broke off suddenly and closed his eyes.

Dawlish looked down at the tired, pale face and wondered whether the strain had been too much for the old man.

Footsteps sounded outside and the murmur of a man's voice.

Pop opened his eyes again.

'Don't know the truth,' he said. 'I think—someone—told Georgette to get her hooks into me. I don't think—they dreamt—I might become serious. Don't blame Georgette for anything until—you can prove it. But I wouldn't be surprised if—friends of hers—couldn't tell you something. Now—Dawlish. I needn't talk about—reward. But help Richard.'

'I will,' promised Dawlish.

'Poor chap! No luck with the girls! Had the devil's own job to get free of Flossie. Met her?'

Dawlish nodded.

'And Phoebe,' said Fairweather. 'Silly couple. But—apart from Richard—my only relatives. Can't forget that. Once in a fit of temper I told them I'd cut them out of my will. I haven't, of course.' He paused, and when he spoke again his voice was stronger. 'Dawlish, am I going to live?'

'The surgeon and the doctors think so,' said Dawlish. 'A lot's up to you.'

He turned as the door was pushed open and the house-surgeon came in.

Dawlish slipped past him, agog to tell Felicity the news, and report to Scotland Yard that Georgette Lee was innocent.

Georgette Lee stepped quickly into Dawlish's Bentley outside Holloway Gaol. She had hardly spoken since the Prison Governor had told her that she was to be freed.

'I am taking you to a friend's flat,' said Dawlish, making her comfortable, 'where you can rest, and decide what you want to do.'

'Will Richard Lloyd be there?'

'No—only my wife and a friend.'

'You're very good,' said Georgette. 'Why?'

'A variety of reasons,' said Dawlish. 'I like to be helpful. I'm curious by nature. I know Pop Fairweather. And Richard asked me to try to prove that you weren't guilty. That's enough, surely?'

'If Pop had died, I'd still be under arrest, I suppose,' she said.

'I think so,' agreed Dawlish.

'So—' She paused.

'I fancy you're thinking along the right lines,' Dawlish said. 'You were to have been framed for his murder, Miss Lee. That's not a nice thought.'

Georgette made no comment.

'I think Richard Lloyd was to have been murdered, too,' Dawlish added quietly.

'You're quite sure that Richard won't be there?'

'You needn't worry at all,' Dawlish assured her. 'Tonight at least you need do nothing but rest. After that, it's up to you. Personally, I think you'd be wise to leave London for a while. If you'd care to go to my home—in Surrey—you'll be very welcome.'

'Thank you,' said Georgette. 'It isn't easy to make plans yet.'

Dawlish pulled into the mews.

'Forget that for the time being,' he said. 'No, don't get out for a moment.'

He opened the door of the car and stepped into the mews. It was very dark. Usually a lamp burned in a wall-bracket, but it was not alight now and Dawlish was puzzled by the gloom. He stepped round to the side of the car, peering about him, before he would allow Georgette to descend.

The hall was in darkness.

As Dawlish switched on the lights Georgette looked about her anxiously. She was nervy, Dawlish thought; she touched his hand and he could feel her trembling.

'Here we are!' Dawlish called out.

He moved to the front room and pushed open the door.

As he did so, Georgette screamed!

A man was standing in the middle of the room, covering Dawlish with a revolver. As Dawlish took a swift glance over his shoulder, he saw a second man emerge from the bedroom, also holding a gun. He seized hold of Georgette's arm with a rough hand.

Dawlish was stupefied.

Less than an hour ago he had left Felicity and Tim here, and he had felt sure that there would be no danger once he and Georgette had reached the flat. Slowly, he began to assess the situation.

Murder was not intended, or they would have fired on sight. They wanted to take Georgette away; *was* there a way of stopping them?

'Don't let them take me!' gasped Georgette. 'I won't go, I won't go!'

Her voice sank to a whisper as the gunman turned savagely towards her.

'Don't move, Dawlish,' said the man from the front room. 'If you try anything I'll shoot.' His voice was harsh; the threat was no idle one.

Dawlish did not move. Looking across the dimly-lit hall towards the man, who had opened the front door, he saw that it was Wilmot He was winding a scarf about Georgette's face, so that she could not scream. That done, he propelled her towards the door. Georgette seemed to be paralyzed with fear. Dawlish, standing quite still, his expression wooden, was conscious of the great threat from both gunmen, yet faced a large issue; he *must* turn the tables on them.

At the back of his mind was another equally grave anxiety; where were Felicity and Tim?

'Out you go,' said Wilmot, pushing Georgette through the hall to the top of the steps.

Suddenly Dawlish lunged forward, and as he did so Wilmot swung round and fired. The bullet missed its target and next moment Dawlish's fist crashed into Wilmot's face. He fell on the inside of the front door. Dawlish leapt over his body and through the door, banging it shut behind him.

Georgette was stumbling down the steps, a shadowy figure in the darkness, sobbing under her breath.

Dawlish cried: 'Get to the other side of the car!' He caught up with her and dragged her with him, past the back of the Bentley.

The front door was wrenched open and the light streamed

into the mews. Two shots rang out and a bullet smashed into the road. Footsteps echoed in the street, and a man shouted in alarm.

Not far away a police whistle shrilled.

'It's all right,' Dawlish called to Georgette. 'You needn't worry any more, it's all right!'

He saw men turning into the mews from the street.

A car rounded a corner some way off and the beam of its headlights flooded the street. The Bentley was close to the wall on one side, but on the other there was room for a small car to pass. He wanted that gap closed, so as to hem the men in.

An idea flashed into Dawlish's mind as the other car drew up.

'Pull in here!' he shouted to the driver. 'Block the end of the mews!'

'What—'

'Block the end of the mews!' roared Dawlish. 'Georgette, go round the corner and wait there for me.'

The driver edged the car a little way forward as Georgette obeyed. A shot rang out and a bullet clanged against the wings of the small car. Another shot hummed past Dawlish's head, and the driver drew in a short, sharp breath and slumped over the wheel.

Dawlish crouched by the side of his Bentley, peering towards the flat. He expected another shot to be fired at any moment; they would shoot as soon as they saw him. He moved forward slowly, still expecting a bullet to come out of the darkness. Then he saw a man spread-eagled and inert on the ground by the side of the stone steps.

'One casualty,' Dawlish murmured. 'All right here!' he called out to the men beyond the cars. 'Go round the back!' He groped about the flagstones for the assailant's gun; then, gun in hand, reached the flat door.

All was silent.

He stepped into the hall. Now that the emergency was past he could think only of Felicity and Tim. If they were not in the bedroom, there was no telling where they might be. He hoped against hope that the assailants had not used their guns on them.

He opened the bedroom door.

Felicity was sitting, bound and gagged in a chair, her eyes wide with fear.

Tim, in the same plight, was lying by the side of the bed.

There had been a ring at the front door bell, Felicity explained, and Tim had opened the door while she had stood waiting—hoping it was Pat and Georgette arriving. A blow over the head had sent Tim reeling back, and the gunmen had silenced Felicity with threats. They had been bundled into the bedroom, and bound and gagged; the door had been locked on them.

Georgette said: 'I'm so sorry. It's all—my fault.'

Felicity laughed rather nervily.

'Oh, Pat's responsible,' she said. 'He's the stormy petrel who brings gunmen and bullets raining down on us.' She looked compassionately at Georgette, much of whose vitality had gone.

Dawlish guessed then that she had been more relieved than sorry to be placed under arrest, having known from the beginning that she was in danger. Doubtless she had had mixed feelings about her release. Now all her energy seemed to have been dissipated.

She had not asked a single question.

Dawlish glanced at Tim, who raised his eyebrows inquiringly. Dawlish nodded towards the door and Tim got up.

JOHN CREASEY

'Come and help me straighten the bedroom, Felicity, will you?' he said, giving her a meaning look as he held the door open for her.

'How long have you been frightened, Georgette?' asked Dawlish, when they were alone. It was the first time he had used her Christian name.

She did not answer.

'It hasn't just started, has it?' asked Dawlish, in a friendly voice. 'You didn't want legal aid, you didn't really care what happened while you were at Holloway. You felt safe there. You were afraid that someone was going to kill you, weren't you?'

She looked at him waveringly, but did not speak.

He said quietly: 'I'm not a policeman, Georgette, and you can tell me things you might not wish to tell the police.'

She stirred uneasily.

'Yes, I've been frightened since that night,' she admitted in a low-pitched voice, 'I realized what they were trying to do, but—I can't *help* you, I don't know very much. I didn't dream anything like this would spring from it.'

'Spring from what?' asked Dawlish.

'From knowing Pop!' she exclaimed. 'Oh, I didn't dream what would happen. I intended only to have a good time and then finish with him—I've done that so many times, you don't need telling!' she added, lifting her hands and dropping them again. 'And the first time I wanted to keep an admirer, he turned me down!' she gave a short laugh. 'Perhaps it wasn't all that important to *me,* but I soon learned it mattered to others.'

'Which others?' Dawlish asked.

She said: 'I'm not really sure, but one of them—'

She broke off abruptly, as she heard a car swing into the mews. Brakes squealed as the car came to a standstill immediately outside the window. Georgette clutched the sides of her chair.

'It's all right, we're surrounded by police,' Dawlish said, reassuringly. 'Georgette, who—'

She was staring towards the window. A car door slammed and a man ran up the steps. He spoke in a harsh voice to the policeman on duty. The front door bell rang and kept on ringing.

Georgette muttered: 'Who is it? Who is it?'

'Probably Richard Lloyd,' said Dawlish. 'Georgette—'

'I don't want to see him!'

'All right, you needn't,' said Dawlish. He could not understand her tension, unless it was that she had been through so much that she dreaded the thought of a difficult interview with Richard. He rose and moved towards the hall.

Tim opened the front door.

'What's all the noise about?' he demanded, testily.

Lloyd snapped: 'I'm told Georgette's here.'

'Oh, it's you,' sniffed Tim. 'I might have known who to expect. Supposing she is. I—'

He broke off as Dawlish opened the door of the sitting-room. Lloyd had brushed Tim to one side and now came towards Dawlish.

'Where's Georgette?' he barked.

'She's resting,' Dawlish said, 'and—'

'I'm going to see her! You're trying to hide her from me, damn you!'

'Don't be an ass,' said Dawlish. 'She's had a pretty rough time, and—'

'She's in there,' said Lloyd, accusingly. 'Let me see her!'

He strode forward but Dawlish made no attempt to move. He could see that the man was livid with fury which was perhaps tinged with fear.

'Later,' said Dawlish.

'If you don't let me see her—' began Lloyd.

'All right, Richard,' called Georgette from the room, 'you'd better come in.'

CHAPTER FOURTEEN

WHO TALKED?

Lloyd went across to Georgette with his arms outstretched. Ignoring the fact that she made no responsive movement he kissed her passionately.

'Oh, my darling, you're safe!'

'I'm—free,' said Georgette.

'You're safe! I'll look after you now,' Lloyd cried. 'We'll get out of London, so that you can have a rest and forget everything. Don't take any notice of Dawlish or the others, they're a pack of scaremongers—no wonder you look worried!'

Dawlish said: 'That's one form of gratitude.'

'Gratitude? What have I to thank you for?' demanded Lloyd. 'I asked you to help and what have you done? Not a damned thing! And when there was trouble you disappeared—you hadn't the nerve to face it. You make me sick!'

Felicity moved a step forward.

Lloyd glanced at her.

'Your wife needn't worry about you running into danger, you know how to look after yourself,' he sneered. 'Georgette, don't take any notice of Dawlish. I don't know what he's been saying, but—'

'If it weren't for Major Dawlish, I should be dead,' said Georgette quietly.

'Nonsense!'

Georgette said: 'It happened half an hour ago.'

Lloyd said stupidly: 'You mean, you've been attacked *since* you left prison?'

'Yes.'

Lloyd turned to Dawlish. His red-rimmed eyes were feverishly bright and his mouth was slack. He said huskily:

'I'm sorry, Dawlish. My nerves have gone to pieces.'

Dawlish looked at him, not unsympathetically.

'Quite so, old chap. Now sit down and have a drink and try to be reasonable. I haven't been raising scares for the sake of it. You and Georgette and your uncle all appear to be in equal danger, but we don't yet know why. I hope we'll find out before long. Until we do, the motto is—*Take Care!*' He poured out a whisky and soda and thrust it into the man's hands.

'But—how did anyone actually *know* she was to be released?'

'Now that,' said Dawlish, 'is what puzzles me. How did *you* know?'

'A reporter told me.'

'When?'

'About half an hour ago,' said Lloyd. 'He rang me up. Gillow was with me—I don't mind admitting I'm fed up with having someone hanging about me all the time. Gillow didn't want me to come round here. I soon told him where to get off,' he added, with a return of his earlier spirit. 'I guessed where she'd be and came over at once.'

'If the Press knew about it, the story would be everywhere,' said Dawlish. 'How well do you know this reporter?'

'Not particularly well,' said Lloyd. 'I'd met him once or twice, and he came to see me when Georgette's flat was burgled. That's where this business began, there isn't any doubt about that. I suppose the police haven't really given that a thought.'

'I think they have,' said Dawlish. 'Now listen to me, Richard. There *is* danger, Georgette won't be safe until we know what all this is about, and until then I think she ought to go down to my home in Surrey and stay there for a week or two. My wife will go with her, and there will be plenty to keep her amused. Any objections?'

Lloyd said uncertainly: 'Well, I—'

'If I may go to Surrey, I'd like that very much,' said Georgette, clinching the matter.

'Then we'll start first thing in the morning,' decided Felicity.

Lloyd was obviously not happy about any plan which parted him from Georgette, but he accepted this one. Once that was agreed, Dawlish made plans for the night. Felicity and Georgette were to stay here, with Tim and Derek, who would be along soon. They would shake-down in the living-room. Dawlish and Lloyd would go to Lloyd's flat—or, Dawlish said, Lloyd could stay there by himself if he really preferred to do so.

Rather sheepishly, Lloyd suggested that it would perhaps be wiser if Dawlish stayed with him.

Georgette rose from her chair and followed Felicity to the door. On the threshold she turned and looked at each of the men in turn, her gaze finally resting on Dawlish.

'I don't think I shall ever be able to thank you,' she said.

Dawlish rubbed his chin; that exit had been worthy of any actress but—*had* it been acting or had it really been sincere? And how much of what she had told him was true?

Lloyd drove off to his flat alone as Dawlish wanted to wait at the mews until Trivett arrived. The Superintendent was in a touchy mood.

'The devil of this job is that we don't even know what we're looking for,' he grumbled. 'It's a series of crimes without a central motive, as far as I can judge. You aren't keeping anything back, are you?'

Dawlish shook his head with bland innocence.

'I just can't see where the crimes tie up with Fairweather,' Trivett went on. 'He said something to you about making enemies, didn't he?'

'Yes. But he's a pretty sick man and he may have been wandering,' Dawlish said.

'Have you any idea why they wanted Georgette?'

'I can make a guess,' said Dawlish. 'I think Georgette first set her cap at Pop because she was told to, and then she fell in love with him—'

'Oh come!'

'I said that I was guessing,' Dawlish reminded him. 'I think that the people who are behind this wanted her to marry him, and when that failed they used violence. So—influence was wanted over Pop, through his wife. There's our starting point.'

Trivett looked at him curiously.

'It could be,' he admitted.

'I think you'll find it is,' said Dawlish. 'They wanted Pop either *in* their hands or *off* their hands. And when it came to murder, it looks as if Lloyd was in the way, too. With Pop alive, Lloyd didn't count for much; with Pop dead, Lloyd would become the man who mattered in *Fairweather Steel* and the other associated businesses. And from there,' went on Dawlish, stifling a yawn, 'it looks to me as if it's a simple step this; now he's not going to have a wife, they want him dead. It starts with Georgette—'

'And she won't talk,' said Trivett, moodily.

'I'm sending her off with Felicity and I think she may talk

to her,' Dawlish said. 'But before she goes, there's one thing I want to be sure of, Bill. How soon did the Press know about Georgette's release?'

'They didn't know, until long after she was here,' said Trivett. 'Of course, it's just possible that someone at the prison may have talked, or a man at the Yard—and news hounds always keep their ears pretty near the ground.'

'I hope no one finds out where Georgette is going,' said Dawlish. 'It wouldn't surprise me if she weren't followed when she leaves in the morning. We ought to make sure that she, and any possible trailer, are under pretty thorough surveillance. You'll look after that, won't you?'

'What time will she be leaving?'

'About ten o'clock—Gillow will drive the girls down.'

'I'll arrange to have your house guarded by the Haslemere police,' promised Trivett, standing up. 'Now I'd better be going, but there's one thing needs saying before I go.'

'Fire away.'

Trivett smiled.

'Whatever you do, don't go off on your own. I can't make head or tail of this business yet, but I do know that it's dangerous You'll keep me informed about anything which crops up, won't you?'

'I will,' promised Dawlish, and went with the Superintendent to the door.

When Trivett had gone Dawlish found that Derek Gillow had arrived and was talking to Tim Jeremy at the top of the steps.

'What did the great man have to say?' he demanded.

'Not very much,' said Dawlish, 'and we aren't any further ahead yet. I'd like you to run Felicity and Georgette down to Haslemere in the morning, Derek. I'm nervous about sending the girls down there alone.'

'Just make me their watchdog and nothing will disturb the even tenor of their lives,' Derek declared.

'You'll be followed by the police and possibly by the enemy, and you'll need to keep a weather eye open.'

'Meaning, take a gun,' concluded Derek.

'I think we'd all be wise to be armed from now on,' Dawlish agreed.

He started up the Bentley's engine, and was soon heading for Lloyd's flat. It was strange how the news of Georgette's release had got out. Yet the more he pondered over it, the more remarkable it seemed that half an hour after he and Georgette had left Holloway, Wilmot and his companion were waiting for them. It suggested earlier information even than the Press could have obtained. *Had* someone been watching the flat and heard him call to Felicity?

He pulled up outside Lloyd's block.

The police were still watching it. Dawlish had a word with a detective officer on duty.

'How long's Mr. Lloyd been in?' asked Dawlish.

'I don't think he is in, sir,' answered the man.

'Oh, he came back an hour ago,' Dawlish told him.

'I didn't see him,' said the detective officer, defensively, 'and I've been here all the time, sir.'

Dawlish hurried upstairs. The flat appeared to be in darkness and there was no answer when he rang the bell. He took out the key Derek had passed over to him, but stood listening intently before he inserted it.

There was no sound.

He turned the key and switched on the hall light. A quick survey assured him that the flat was empty. In the living-room two ash-trays were filled with ash and cigarette butts, and there was a burnt-out cigarette lying on a small telephone table, one which Lloyd had doubtless put down when he had answered the telephone call informing him of Georgette's release.

He was standing there wondering what it could mean when the telephone bell, harsh and insistent, rang through the empty flat.

He lifted the receiver quickly.

'Dawlish speaking,' he said, and expected to hear Lloyd speak.

Instead he heard a familiar voice, which held a note of laughter in it.

'I guessed you'd be there,' said 'Max', 'and I just rang through to tell you that you needn't wait up for Lloyd. We're looking after him. And if you'd like a chat with him or with us, be at Hammersmith Broadway, by the station, at one o'clock tomorrow.'

Before Dawlish could reply, the line went dead.

After telephoning Trivett, Dawlish looked about the flat. In a bedside cupboard he found a hypodermic syringe and a tiny box of phials containing morphia.

It made him both worried and thoughtful.

This, then, could be the reason for Lloyd's over-wrought nerves and near-hysteria.

Before leaving the flat he very carefully replaced the syringe and the box of phials in the exact place in which he had found them.

CHAPTER FIFTEEN

'MAX' AGAIN

Dawlish watched Felicity and Georgette depart next day with certain misgivings. Since Lloyd had disappeared it was possible that he would be persuaded to talk and that Max and 'the Boss' knew where Georgette would be. The Haslemere police had promised to keep a close watch on the house, however, and there seemed little likelihood of anything going amiss on the road.

Dawlish turned to Tim.

'The beginning of the final stage, I think,' he remarked.

'You mean, you're making a blind guess,' retorted Tim.

Dawlish chuckled.

'Could be. Now listen: we've a job on hand.' He told Tim about the appointment at Hammersmith Broadway.

Tim's eyes glistened.

'You didn't tell Bill Trivett, did you?'

'I did not,' said Dawlish. 'This is our chicken. We won't go together of course . . .'

He talked for another five minutes, to Tim's evident satisfaction.

*   *   *

Hammersmith Broadway was a good place for such a meeting. Traffic flowed from the five roads in what seemed an unending stream. Dawlish stood, tense and expectant, by the main entrance to the Underground.

On the other side of the road, at the wheel of a small, borrowed car, sat Tim Jeremy. Dawlish had hired a drive-yourself Lagonda which had a fine turn of speed. It was parked round the corner.

Tall men passed by the dozen, but Max did not put in an appearance. By ten past one, Dawlish began to feel annoyed. Five minutes later he was just beginning to think that Max had changed his mind, when suddenly he saw Bert May. Dawlish looked at him blankly, hoping that the little man would not give away the fact that they knew each other; it was impossible to guess who would be watching them.

Bert looked away, but edged towards him.

It flashed through Dawlish's mind that he might have been sent by Max. He waited until Bert reached the shop window by which he was standing.

Dawlish caught the words.

'Anything doing?'

'Why are you here?' Dawlish asked, speaking out of the side of his mouth; his lips hardly moved.

'Looking for a lanky pole with a grin,' muttered Bert.

No one could have described Max more aptly.

'What's the name of the man you're looking for?'

'Don't know. He was pointed out to me.'

'What about the people who called at *The Pines*?'

'None I know,' said Bert, deprecatingly. 'But I've remembered two more who called at Georgie Lee's house. Worth a quid each?'

'Yes.'

'Len Morgan,' said Bert, casting a quick, nervous glance over his shoulder. 'A nasty piece of work with friends in the West End. The other was Flossie, the girl at *The Pines*.'

'Ah,' exclaimed Dawlish.

He took two pound notes from his pocket and, as Bert passed him, slipped them into his ready hand. Bert moved on, looking about him again with an anxious gaze.

It was now twenty-five minutes past one, and there was no sign of 'Max'.

Dawlish turned and walked towards his car. Max may have discovered that someone else was waiting for him, and decided not to come. Dawlish pondered over this. At one time, it had seemed as if he and the police were dealing with only one set of people; now the evidence that there were two parties seemed inescapable. There were 'the Boss' and Max on the one hand, and the men who employed Bert on the other.

As he reached the Lagonda, a man appeared from the side entrance to the station. It was Max. He came up to Dawlish at once.

'Ready for a journey?'

'How far?'

'Just beyond Staines.'

'Shall I follow you?' asked Dawlish.

'You'd better take me,' Max said, 'I didn't bring a car.' He peered about him as they got into the Lagonda.

'Looking for someone?'

'I certainly am. A little customer wearing a red ribbon,' said Max. 'I was warned that he would probably be following me, and I don't want to be seen.' As the Lagonda moved off Max said abruptly: 'I'm glad you came. The Boss wants to see you. If the police hadn't been too near the house yesterday this wouldn't have been necessary. We had to leave in a hurry.'

'I see,' said Dawlish.

'We picked up Lloyd because we wanted a talk with him,' said Max, 'but we've come to the conclusion that he doesn't know much. I don't think Fairweather trusted him with a great deal, do you?'

'I don't know.'

'Anyway, we released Lloyd this morning,' Max said.

'That's fine,' said Dawlish.

'There's one thing I can tell you now,' Max went on. 'Wilmot has been playing a double game—working with us and with another crowd who have it in for Fairweather. And Wilmot was pretty vicious about you, Dawlish. If he gets a chance, he'll kill you.' He spoke quite calmly.

'I'd guessed that,' said Dawlish. 'Who are these other people?'

'I don't really know,' Max assured him, 'except that they wear a red ribbon. I don't think the Boss knows a great deal, either. I've been trailed by one of the beggars this morning, but shook him off near Hammersmith. You weren't followed by the police, were you?' Max glanced anxiously behind him.

Reassured he sank back in his seat, speaking only to direct Dawlish where to go. The country became more open and lonely and presently they reached some crossroads, with a dilapidated signpost; the sign on the left read: *Dingly Farm.*

'That's where we're going,' Max volunteered, 'but we'll turn down the next lane, it's more concealed.'

The lane proved to be narrow and winding, heavily ridged by farm tractors. The Lagonda lurched from side to side and Dawlish had to give full attention to his driving. Before long Dingly Farm came into view. The farmhouse was a sorry sight at closer quarters. The windows were broken, the outhouses were obviously in need of attention and the only signs of life were a few scrawny fowls which pecked and scratched in the dirt of the yard.

'A little shabby, it's true, but it's much better inside than it is out,' said Max airily, getting out of the car.

A small car was moving, a long way off. Max waited until it had passed the end of the lane.

'That's all right,' he said. 'There isn't much traffic along here, and I was afraid we'd been spotted. Nervous, Dawlish?'

'Very,' said Dawlish, drily.

'I wonder why no one's about,' Max commented. 'I expected someone to be on the lookout for us.' He opened the front door and they stepped into a wide, stone-flagged hall. 'Anyone about?' he called out.

There was no reply.

'It looks as if they've been called away,' Max said. 'Wait here a few minutes, will you?'

'Have I a choice?' asked Dawlish.

'We're not going to keep you here against your will this time,' Max assured him.

As he went out, Dawlish turned to the window. There was a thick coverage of trees nearby, and he felt sure that Tim was hiding there. He would have driven his car past the turning to the farmhouse, in order not to arouse suspicion.

It was comforting to feel that help was close by.

Not that there seemed the slightest cause for alarm. Max's attitude was puzzling, but it was clear enough that he was either deeply disturbed at finding the farmhouse deserted—or else pretended to be. Dawlish reserved judgment, and waited patiently, fingering the small automatic in his pocket.

Yes, it was a queer business altogether, and—

Something crashed overhead! It shook the ceiling from which the powdery plaster fell in small flakes. Dawlish swung round towards the door.

Silence fell upon the house.

CHAPTER SIXTEEN

'THE BOSS'

Dawlish moved swiftly and quietly along the passage, towards the foot of the staircase. He could hear nothing. Had Max fallen and injured himself? If so, he might have lost consciousness, which would explain the silence. Or had he too been subjected to one of the surprise attacks so favoured by the men who were concerned in this affair?

Dawlish heard nothing as he leapt silently up the stairs. At the top was a narrow landing at the end of which was an open door. Dawlish made haste towards it. Max was standing at the far side of the room, staring at something that lay at his feet.

Coming closer Dawlish saw that it was the body of a dead man.

In spite of the injuries, Dawlish recognized 'The Boss'.

Dawlish bent over the body, shocked by the brutality which had been wreaked.

Max spoke at last.

'He was in—in the cupboard,' he said huskily.

'I see,' said Dawlish. It was easy to realize that the moment

Max had opened the cupboard the dead man's body had thudded to the floor. He touched a lifeless hand.

'He—he's dead all right,' Max said. 'There's no point in touching him.'

Dawlish straightened up and looked steadily at the man who had brought him here.

Max's lean face had gone very pale. His eyes were unnaturally bright and he seemed unable to look anywhere but at the victim.

Dawlish remembered Georgette as she had been at Tim's flat on the previous night—hopeless, frightened, subdued—as if not greatly caring what happened to her. Now, if appearances were any guide, Max felt just as she had felt.

Dawlish said: 'This won't do!' He went to the silent man, took his arm and guided him downstairs. Pushing open the door of what appeared to be a dining-room, he found a bottle of whisky and some glasses. He poured out a stiff drink and thrust it into Max's hand.

Max took the glass indifferently, and raised it to his lips. He swallowed a little, hesitated, and then tossed the drink down. It seemed to change his dejection to fury. Half-sobbing he cried out:

'I'll get them, I'll smash their heads in if it's the last thing I do. To kill *him*! I'll hunt them down, one by one. I'll make them wish they'd never been born!'

He raised his clenched fists towards the ceiling, his eyes blazing. Watching him, there seemed to Dawlish to be something unreal about this outburst. Like 'the Boss' himself, it did not seem quite natural.

That thought passed in a flash.

'How many men were there?' he asked.

'Two.' Max turned towards the window. 'I didn't trust them— and he didn't, either. Like Wilmot, they were double-crossing us. One of them did this, I don't think there's much doubt about that.'

'Do you know where to find them?' Dawlish asked.

'I'll find them all right,' said Max, savagely. 'But I suppose we'd better look round here, first.'

Together, they searched every room in the farmhouse, but found no sign of the other men who had remained with 'The Boss'.

Alone for a moment, Dawlish crossed to a window over-looking the copse, and waved, hoping that Tim would see him.

Downstairs, Max was waiting in the kitchen, dour, uncommunicative.

'Look here, Max, it's no use taking it like this: sulking won't help. The police will have to be called as soon as possible and we've got to decide what to do with you. If you don't stay to face them, you'll be suspected of this murder—you know that, don't you?'

Max looked up with cold, unfriendly eyes.

'I'm on the run already,' he said. 'If you think you're going to keep me here—'

'I'll keep you here if I think it's necessary,' Dawlish said. 'I don't want to—but I do want the answers to some questions the police will ask. What time did you leave here this morning?'

'Just before eleven,' muttered Max. 'I left him and the other two—'

'Who were they?'

'Sidney and Harrison,' Max said, making a great effort to speak clearly. 'They joined us about the same time as Wilmot. I never really—trusted them. The only man I could trust was "The Boss"—'

'Although he was on the run?'

Max said: 'Sit down, Dawlish, I'd better talk to you. I can't leave it to him now.' He tossed his cigarette into the fireplace, and began to speak in a low-pitched, bitter voice.

He talked for twenty minutes without ceasing. Dawlish did not interrupt him; and, when it was over, did not question him.

He said: 'Thanks, Max. I think I can see the situation more clearly. But we still have to decide what to do with you.'

'I'll look after myself, thanks.'

Dawlish said: 'No, it isn't quite so easy as that. I'm going to tell the police the whole story, and I'll have to mention your part. You can't keep on the run for ever,' he added as Max began to protest. 'If you've told me the truth you haven't much to worry about. But if the police have to hunt for you, it'll be a different story.'

Max said: 'I'm going after his murderers.'

'Not yet,' said Dawlish. 'That's for the police.'

Max jumped up.

'Damn you, and damn the police! You've said yourself that they'll probably think I killed him—a fat chance I'd have of getting free if I give myself up. Don't move!' He snatched an automatic from his pocket and pointed it at Dawlish. 'Stay where you are!'

Dawlish sat back in his chair and looked at him steadily.

'You're being very foolish,' he said.

Max backed towards the door.

'I don't want to harm you, Dawlish, I don't want any trouble, but I warn you that if you come any nearer I'll shoot.' He stretched out his left arm for the door and pulled it open.

'I rather think not,' came Tim Jeremy's deep voice.

Max swung round.

Tim caught the man's wrist and twisted it; the gun dropped. He pushed the astonished Max into the room, and turned to Dawlish.

'I thought the semaphoring meant that you wanted help,' he said.

Max cried: 'Dawlish, you double-crossing swine, if I'd known—'

Tim stooped down and picked up Max's gun.

'You really shouldn't go about with nasty little things like this,' he said reprovingly. 'What next, Pat?'

Dawlish said: 'I'm trying to think of a quiet spot where you could take Max for a few hours and make sure that he doesn't do anything foolish, while I tell the police what's happened.' He looked at the lean-faced man thoughtfully.

'What about your uncle's place at Guildford? And I could get one or two of the boys to go along and keep Maxie company.'

Max swung round on Dawlish.

'You can't do this!' he cried. 'I've got to find Sidney and Harrison, I've got to make them pay for—'

'That's the trouble,' Dawlish said. 'You won't keep out of mischief. Take him to Pinkie's, Tim. If I haven't telephoned the old boy before you arrive, tell him I'll be getting through soon. And Max—' his face was serious and his voice hard—'you'll be all right provided you don't make a nuisance of yourself. I'll do the best I can for you with the police.'

'You'll regret this, Dawlish!'

'I hope neither of us will,' said Dawlish, gravely. 'Think you can handle him, Tim?'

With Max walking, under protest, a little way ahead, and Tim keeping his right hand in his coat pocket, the two men walked towards the thicket, where Tim's car was parked.

Dawlish thought of Max's story; and of Trivett.

A little more than two hours later, Trivett was sitting in the parlour of the farmhouse. The Staines police had been on duty at the house for some time, after Dawlish had telephoned Scotland Yard. Photographs had been taken and tests for fingerprints had been made, and 'The Boss's' body was now on the way to the mortuary. Dawlish had already given a Staines Inspector and Trivett some details of events—including his appointment with Max. He gave them to understand that Max had escaped from the farmhouse, but told Trivett the truth.

Trivett looked at him narrowly.

'That was a damn fool thing to do. He might get away.'

'Of course he might,' said Dawlish. 'But you shouldn't have too much trouble picking him up again.'

'Why the devil did you do it?'

'To learn more about Max's real make-up,' Dawlish said. 'Anyhow, he'll have to be smart to escape from Tim.'

Trivett growled: 'You'll have a job explaining this to the A.C., but never mind it now. You say Max told you a story?'

'An interesting one, Bill,' said Dawlish. 'I've been trying to decide whether to believe it or not.' He paused a moment and then went on in a quiet voice: 'According to Max, his "Boss" was at one time a director of the Fairweather's steel company. The two men fell out. Fairweather was vindictive. There was some talk about the manufacture and supply of armaments for foreign countries. According to Max, the other man wouldn't agree, but Fairweather was quite prepared to do business—'

'Now look here,' protested Trivett, 'it's impossible to export arms without a licence—'

'Oh, the deals went through Fairweather's foreign interests,' said Dawlish. 'All legal and above board, although according to Max it wouldn't have done Fairweather's reputation any good had the facts been made public. Also according to Max, Fairweather was aware of the danger, and set a trap for "The

Boss", whose name Max refused to tell me. You'll get it soon enough, if the story's true.'

Trivett said: 'Go on.'

'The trap was a simple one and "The Boss" fell into it,' said Dawlish. 'As a result, he had to resign his position as director and the police have been looking for him for some years. He disguised himself, helped by plastic surgery, and he's been living a secluded life. But, if Max is to be believed, he has been determined from the beginning to stop Fairweather's traffic in arms. He couldn't come out into the open, so he employed Max—who worked for him at *Fairweather's* and was still in the old man's employ—to dig out what information he could. Max was caught prying, and was fired. After that, "The Boss" decided that it was time to try to scare the old man into doing what he wanted. Threats were frequently made, and Fairweather was harassed in every way. And, to do the job properly, "The Boss" employed two or three thugs, including Wilmot, to give point to these threats. But little was actually achieved because "The Boss" discovered a second party working against Fairweather.'

Trivett looked at Dawlish without favour.

'It seems a pretty tall story.'

'Tall enough,' Dawlish agreed, 'But whether that makes it untrue or not I wouldn't like to say. And I'm passing on exactly what Max told me, remember.'

Trivett nodded.

'The offence which "The Boss" committed was that of transferring assets to America,' said Dawlish. 'According to Max, Fairweather faked certificates of authority and afterwards took the fakes away—so that it *looked* as if "The Boss" had been salting away assets for some time. "The Boss" knew he would be thought guilty, that's why he ducked for cover. For the rest— Max says that he doesn't know the identity of the other people who are working against Fairweather, but knows they've bribed Wilmot and the strongarm men. He's sure that they killed "The Boss". I'm not going to say whether I think it's likely or not,' Dawlish went on, 'but there's the story. And it does give us one thing—a possible motive for the attacks on Fairweather.'

Trivett said: 'Meaning?'

'A means to implement blackmail,' Dawlish said lightly. 'And it gives you another lead, Bill—a chance to investigate Fairweather's affairs more closely. I think you've a good enough excuse now, don't you?'

'I suppose we have,' agreed Trivett, 'although I doubt whether Fairweather has left any loose ends. *I* think that Max told you a cock-and-bull story and that you were a fool not to hold him here.'

'Max on his own isn't going to do much harm,' Dawlish argued.

'Possibly not,' Trivett said, rising from his chair, 'but his story does nothing to make the affair less obscure. You said the other day that the whole business started with Georgette—but Georgette wasn't in it right at the beginning.'

Dawlish grinned.

'Now, Bill! I meant that the first attempt by the unknown crooks was through Georgette, I wasn't thinking of the history of Fairweather's rackets, if any. Be fair! I think that I'll drive over and see that young woman,' he added. 'Felicity might have learned something from her by now. Okay?'

'I can't stop you,' Trivett said.

'I don't know why you should want to. I may get a lot out of Georgette. I'll let you know if I do.'

'Perhaps,' growled Trivett, sceptically.

Dawlish waved a cheerful farewell, and left the farmhouse a little after half past four. When he reached Staines he telephoned his uncle's house and was told that his 'friends' had been made welcome. He drove quickly from Staines to Guildford and took the Portsmouth Road for Haslemere. Seeing Georgette had not been among his original plans, but he had found himself thinking a great deal about her.

The sun was warm, the countryside a delight, and as he drew near his home Dawlish wished that the whole affair were over; that he could return to his house and orchard and forget matters of violence. Trivett had the curious idea that he really enjoyed such affairs . . .

He could never make up his mind whether Trivett was right!

As he swung round the last corner to *Four Ways,* he saw a man standing by a car and looking disconsolately at the engine. Dawlish slowed down, intending to offer help, but suddenly he trod on the accelerator.

He saw a tiny piece of red ribbon in the man's buttonhole; but that was not all.

He had seen the man before—plump, self-assured and cheerful. It was Cooper, the 'drunk' motorist who had driven into Lloyd's car—and whose licence had been suspended.

CHAPTER SEVENTEEN

INTEREST IN *FOUR WAYS*

So his house was being watched.

Dawlish turned thoughtfully into the drive. *Four Ways* was a charming, half-timbered house with a pleasant orchard, and a small market garden beyond. Dawlish saw with some relief that two policemen and a man in plainclothes were unobtrusively moving through the trees.

Felicity heard the car approach and waved from a first floor window. By the time Dawlish reached the porch, she had opened the front door.

'Darling, you didn't say you were coming!'

'I couldn't stay away another minute,' Dawlish told her, laughing.

'You mean you want to talk to Georgette,' retorted Felicity.

'I may be able to fit that in,' agreed Dawlish. With his arm about her waist, they went into the hall. 'How is she?'

'Still very quiet.'

'She hasn't told you anything?'

'No, and if she ever does it must be in her own time and way.'

'You're quite right. How's Derek?'

Felicity shot him a curious glance.

'In the garden with Georgette.'

The tone of her voice made Dawlish raise his eyebrows.

'Like that, is it?'

'I'm afraid so. Does it matter?'

'It's a complication we didn't want,' said Dawlish, 'but I don't know that it matters a great deal. Odd how they fall for Georgette, isn't it?'

'Is it so odd?' asked Felicity.

Dawlish said in comic despair: 'Not you too!'

'I've come to like her very much,' Felicity said stoutly. 'It isn't her looks or her manner; there's something about her that I can't help admiring. I can easily understand men falling for her, even Pop Fairweather. How is he?'

'Still progressing favourably,' said Dawlish, absently. 'Well, well! If Lloyd arrives and thinks that Derek is not sticking strictly to business—'

'Has *he* turned up again?'

'I'm told that he was released by my friend Max, so I expect he'll be along shortly,' Dawlish said.

'Oh,' said Felicity. 'You know, I find that man rather a trial.'

'I could think of a stronger word,' suggested Dawlish. 'Have you had tea?'

'How guileless—or do I mean devious?' laughed Felicity. 'I'll get you some.'

She left him with a wave of her hand, while Dawlish strayed to his favourite armchair, thinking again about Cooper, whose presence meant that the 'other people' knew where Georgette was: either she had been followed—but Trivett had not mentioned the car being trailed on the journey—or someone had told them where to find her.

Who had told them Georgette was at *Four Ways*?

Lloyd had known, of course, and Lloyd had been a prisoner—

He began to feel uneasy about Lloyd.

True, Max had told him that the young man had been released that morning, and there seemed nothing to worry about; but it was not wise to assume that Max had told the truth. Trivett had heard nothing from Lloyd, and it was surely likely that as soon as he was free the man would get in touch with the authorities.

Dawlish rubbed his chin.

He heard Georgette's voice outside, and Derek's answering her. The couple wandered in from the garden. Georgette was smiling—and she looked much less strained and careworn than on the previous night.

Had Felicity not warned him, Dawlish might not have noticed the particular way Derek was looking at her.

'Hallo, folk!' he greeted lazily.

'We heard you were here,' Derek grinned, 'And hastened to pay homage. Anything doing?'

'Nothing much,' Dawlish said, 'but there's a plump Johnny with a car near the gates. He's got a red ribbon in his buttonhole, which, in itself, is somewhat fishy. Go and get a good look at him, will you?'

As Derek hurried off, Georgette turned to Dawlish.

'I have been waiting for you to come because there are several things I want to tell you,' she said nervously. 'Richard won't come today, will he?' She seemed anxious.

'I don't think so,' said Dawlish.

'I was going to tell you last night,' she began slowly. 'I started to say that when Pop turned me down, others were angry about it. It seems so—nightmarish, sometimes I can hardly believe that it really happened and yet—it *did*, Major Dawlish.'

'Yes,' murmured Dawlish.

'The first time I met Pop I was with some rather gay and thoughtless friends who wagered that I wouldn't be able to persuade Pop to take me out one evening. I accepted the challenge, and was introduced to him, and—'

'You won hands down!'

Georgette smiled.

'It wasn't difficult! And the same friend offered me a hundred pounds to a shilling if I could keep him interested for a month. *That* was fairly easy, too. But it was all a joke at first. Only when I got to know Pop did I realize that—well, I liked him. When I found that he was taking it seriously I wasn't too happy about it. My friends were—well, to them it *was* a joke. You can imagine what they said—what it was like. I felt that I was cheating him, and I somehow didn't *want* to cheat Pop Fairweather.'

'I see,' said Dawlish.

'At the end of the month my friend paid the hundred pounds,' Georgette went on. 'I needed it. I was nearly broke, and I wouldn't take any money from Pop—not at first, anyhow,' she added, a little awkwardly. 'Next, this friend offered me five hundred pounds to a penny that I couldn't make Pop propose within three months. You see, he was looking on it as a joke—or I thought he was— and I needed the money. So I accepted. The three months were up two days ago,' she added, 'and when it was beginning to look as if I wasn't going to win, my friend came along and suggested that I should stage the—the burglary at my flat!'

Dawlish said mildly: 'Yes, that was fairly obvious.'

'I—I knew it was foolish,' she admitted, 'and I didn't want to go on with it, but I had to. Then suddenly Richard became difficult, and Pop swung right round. I—I was miserable, and sickened by it all. And then, for the first time, I found that my friend had a reason for what he'd done. He *wanted* me to marry

Pop. And you see, I—I had to do what he wanted as far as I could. He—'

Dawlish murmured: 'He'd been blackmailing you.'

'I wondered if you would guess,' Georgette said slowly. 'Yes, I'd let myself get into a position where he *could* blackmail me. But I didn't realize how serious it was until the day Pop was attacked. My—my friend lost his temper and threatened to *kill* him. I thought it was wild talk, but I was sufficiently scared to decide that Richard and Pop should be told about it. I was there when Pop was attacked,' she went on. 'I'd waited there for half-an-hour, left a note for Richard and was going out when the front-door bell rang. Before I knew what had happened a scarf was tied round my head just—just as it was last night.'

Dawlish nodded; she was talking in a low-pitched, nervous voice now.

'They locked me in a cloakroom,' she told him. 'I heard Pop come in, and I heard them go for him. When it was over, they made me handle the iron ornament they'd used, and then they let me go home. I was so frightened that I didn't know what to do. When the police came it was almost a relief. I felt safer in prison than at the mercy of those men.' She paused, then moved to the window, every movement easy and graceful.

'I don't expect I shall be allowed to live very long,' she said calmly.

'I think we'll see you through,' Dawlish commented in a cheerful voice, 'we're quite used to blocking attempts at murder, you know. And that's the whole story?'

She nodded, without looking at him.

'There are two questions I must ask,' Dawlish said, a little diffidently. 'I hope you'll answer them. What hold has your friend got over you, Georgette?'

She did not answer at once. He waited, sensing the turmoil in her mind.

She turned and looked at him.

'I'm married, Major Dawlish. Pop suspected it, I think.'

Afterwards, Dawlish wondered why he had been so surprised. He forced himself to think about the implications of Georgette's statement. What harm would it do her if it were known that she was married?

She said quietly: 'You are thinking that it isn't a secret of much importance, but—if you take the trouble to think about the way I've lived, you'll realize that if it were known, I—well, men wouldn't *want* to marry me, I'd just be fair game.' She caught her breath. 'I've fooled *dozens* of men, who've begged me to marry them. Over the years I've become frightened in case the truth leaked out. Perhaps vanity, and fear of looking a fool, had something to do with it. And—and I was ashamed of my husband. I haven't lived with him for twenty years, and very few people know. Only Len ever talked to me about it.'

'Len?' asked Dawlish, quickly.

'Len Morgan,' she said. 'I'm frightened of him. He told me on the night that Pop was attacked that if I gave him away I wouldn't live much longer. I—I knew that he was a rogue, but I didn't think he was a murderer. I didn't dream of murder or violence.' She paused, closing her eyes.

Dawlish said quietly: 'This Len Morgan has blackmailed you for some time, hasn't he?'

'Yes. If—if he knew I'd told you his name—'

'I shouldn't worry too much about that,' said Dawlish. 'He must have felt fairly sure that you would keep silent, or he wouldn't have let the police arrest you.'

'I've never been able to understand that,' admitted Georgette.

'But then, I've been too terrified for any of it to make sense to me. My husband, Bert—'

Dawlish said in a sharp voice: 'Did you say *Bert*?'

'Yes.'

'Bert *May*?'

Georgette jumped up.

'Do you know him?' she exclaimed.

'We've met,' Dawlish said very slowly.

'Well, he's my husband. *Now* do you understand why I was ashamed?'

CHAPTER EIGHTEEN

THE *GO-GETTER*

Dawlish sat in the drawing-room of *Four Ways,* watching Felicity, Georgette and Derek walking in the garden. A laugh rang out suddenly, deep and natural.

Derek had not seen Cooper. From the man's disappearance, it was assumed that he had been waiting only to report whether and when Dawlish arrived. Dawlish had telephoned to Trivett about Cooper as soon as Derek had returned.

Up to that time, Lloyd had not shown up at his flat.

Dawlish rubbed the back of his head gingerly.

In some ways the situation was easy to understand, in others he could not make head or tail of it. It seemed almost fantastic that Georgette had allowed the man Morgan to influence her so strongly, and yet—it was easy enough to understand when one remembered Georgette's character. He did not think there was any serious doubt that Georgette had told the truth about her own feelings and actions—and she had been ashamed in the curiously childlike way which was part of her attractiveness.

Dawlish imagined the tortuous twists of thought which had made her keep silent although she knew that Morgan had framed her for the assault on Pop—but beyond that Dawlish could not understand what had happened.

How *could* Morgan have felt safe with her in the hands of the police? What on earth had possessed him to send her home to await arrest? Under interrogation she might so easily have broken down and named him. Morgan must have lived in an agony of suspense.

It was easy enough to see why he had tried to kidnap her; but why not kill her? And *why* had he allowed the police to arrest her? Further, why did Morgan want to kill Pop?

One thing had certainly gone badly wrong with the man's plans. Pop had not died. That in itself would have been enough to make Morgan hide, but—

Dawlish still boggled at the other unexplained fact.

'*Why?*' he asked aloud, and jumped to his feet. 'It just doesn't make sense!' He went to the telephone and put in a call to Trivett's flat. He answered at once. 'Hallo, Bill,' said Dawlish. 'Anything turned up your end?'

'Nothing fresh,' said Trivett. 'What about yours?'

'Odds and ends of information, including the fact that Georgette's married—Bill, what do you know about a man named Len Morgan?'

Trivett said slowly: 'We suspect that he's in a dozen different rackets, and we've been trying to catch him for years, but he's always kept one jump ahead of us. Why are you interested?'

'I've a feeling that Georgette's frightened of him,' Dawlish said.

'That wouldn't surprise me.'

'Have you seen him lately?' asked Dawlish.

'Not for several days.'

'Do you know where I can find him now?' asked Dawlish.

'I know several places where you might get him,' said Trivett. 'But if you think there's any reason for hauling him in—'

'Not for the moment,' Dawlish said convincingly. 'But there's always the future. If I come up to town right away will you tell me as much as you can?'

'All right.'

'Thanks! There's just one other thing,' continued Dawlish. 'Just how strong was your case against Georgette?'

'It seemed unbreakable,' said Trivett, after a pause. He uttered a dry laugh. 'I think we arrived just in time to save her life, Pat.'

'In what way?'

'She had some morphine tablets in an aspirin bottle by the side of her bed, and if she'd taken a couple she wouldn't have woken up next morning,' said Trivett.

'I see,' said Dawlish, thoughtfully.

'And I can tell you something else—' began Trivett.

'I know it,' said Dawlish. 'You think Pop may have lied to save her.'

'I'm beginning to think so,' Trivett said.

'And you may be right,' conceded Dawlish. ''Bye.'

He replaced the receiver as the others came into the hall. What had seemed inexplicable was now easily explained. Morgan had sent her home and had put morphine tablets by the side of her bed. She would almost certainly have taken 'aspirins' that night, to induce sleep—and it would have looked as if she had committed suicide. Morgan had made the mistake of leaving it to her to take the tablets—he had banked on what had seemed a winner.

Georgette was certainly lucky to be alive.

Dawlish arrived at the top of a flight of narrow, darkened stairs. A little man with a long nose peered at him from behind a grille. From a room nearby came the sound of tinny music and the shuffle of people dancing. This was the

Go-Getter, one of Len Morgan's more recently acquired business interests.

'Good evening,' said Dawlish to the man with the long nose. The other sniffed.

''Evening.'

'Am I too late?' asked Dawlish.

'Depends.' The man sniffed again. 'Member?'

'Not exactly, I rather hoped to have a word with Len Morgan.'

''E's not in town.'

'I was told I might find him here,' said Dawlish with an air of innocent persistence. 'I've a message for him.'

'Dunno when he'll be back,' said the other.

His little eyes peered at Dawlish suspiciously; Dawlish seemed to have seen a dozen such suspicious faces during the past two hours. This was his fifth call at a nightclub in the quest for Len Morgan.

'When was he last here?' asked Dawlish.

The little man's eyes narrowed, and he glanced over his shoulder. The dance music grew louder as a door opened. A man appeared in the hall. He was tall and sleek, with a swarthy face, handsome in a dark, un-English way. He did not approach Dawlish but stood listening; and Dawlish thought that probably the little man had signalled for him. Such a place as the *Go-Getter* would be well-provided with a bell-alarm system.

''E left town a week ago.'

'And there isn't any way I can get a message to him?' asked Dawlish, simulating distress.

The dark man stepped forward. Dawlish saw that his dress suit—too soft, too slinky—was of exaggerated cut, and his eyes were hard and wary.

'Who is it the gentleman wants, Sam?' he asked.

Dawlish turned to look more fully at him.

'I've an urgent message for Mr. Len Morgan. I know he would be grateful if it could reach him. You don't happen to know where I could find him, do you?'

'I could take the message,' said the swarthy man smoothly.

Dawlish allowed his face to fall.

'Oh, dear,' he said. 'I don't think I could pass it on by a third party. I'm sure she wouldn't like that.'

'She?'

'Er—my friend, yes,' said Dawlish.

The other said easily: 'I could try to get the message to him—but if I don't know what it is, that doesn't get us far.'

'Too true,' said Dawlish. He bit his lips. 'I—well, I'd better have a talk with my friend. She'll tell me what to do.' He smiled ingratiatingly. 'You might let me know if Mr. Morgan *should* come back—I'll call in again. The—er—the truth is, I think—er—he would be grateful if he were to get the message. Well, thanks. Good night.'

Dawlish left the *Go-Getter* slowly, guessing that he would be followed.

For the first time that night he felt that he was getting results. He decided that Morgan had been building up an alibi, so that if Georgette did name him and he were caught, he would have a chance to discredit her evidence.

He reached Piccadilly Circus, and while waiting for a stream of traffic to pass, looked round casually.

Out of the corner of his eye he saw the swarthy man standing a few yards away. Dawlish crossed into Regent Street and then took a short cut to Piccadilly. He did not think there was any likelihood of an attack here, but it was as well to be prepared.

He reached Piccadilly, and turned right.

The swarthy man was drawing closer.

Dawlish walked to Tim's flat at a sharper pace, and the other kept close behind. At the entrance to the mews, Dawlish paused. A policeman loomed out of the darkness, and recognized him.

'Everything O.K., sir?'

'Yes, thanks,' said Dawlish. 'I'm expecting a visitor—he's quite harmless.'

'I'll just stand by then, sir,' said the policeman and retired to his point of vantage in a doorway.

Dawlish began to mount the steps.

Next moment, he heard Tim Jeremy's voice.

'Hallo, hallo, there!'

'Tim, you ass!'

'Well, I like that,' protested Tim. 'I get off the sofa to open the door to you, and you tell me I'm an ass. I mean to say, old chap, it's a bit too much. Coming or going?' he added.

Dawlish stepped into the hall.

'There's a johnny down there,' Tim whispered. 'Just turned the corner.'

'He'll probably call,' Dawlish said. He waited until the door was shut, and then asked eagerly: 'What have you done with Max?'

'No Max,' said Tim, sadly. 'I rang you at *Four Ways*, but you'd just left.'

'What happened?'

'All went well until we got to Pinkie's. I think Pinkie's reputation upset him. Being a J.P. and suchlike. It got him down. I couldn't lock him in his room very well, Pinkie would have thought it odd—he thought it fishy in any case—and Maxie slipped out. I had an idea you half-expected it.'

'I did,' said Dawlish.

They waited in the stillness of the flat as footsteps sounded on the steps.

'Do I let him in?' Tim demanded.

'Yes. I've been looking for a man named Morgan and inquired

for him at the *Go-Getter*. This merchant's followed me from there. Act the fool a bit.'

'My most natural role,' Tim said with relish.

The footsteps ceased and the bell rang. Tim allowed a decent interval to elapse and then went to open the door. The swarthy-faced man said politely:

'Good evening. May I see your—er—friend?'

'*See* him? Well, I don't know. But I could ask—and your name?'

'Mr. Smith,' said the swarthy man.

'Oh, *Smith*. He's very friendly with all the Smiths,' said Tim brightly. 'Do come in. Pat!' he called. 'Mr. Smith wants to see you.'

He led the way into the front room.

Dawlish looked up at him from the depths of an armchair, and raised a hand in greeting.

'Why, hallo!'

'Good evening. I'm sorry I'm so late, but I thought I might be able to help you.'

'Help?' echoed Dawlish. 'Thoughtful of you, but do I need help?'

'You were inquiring for Mr. Len Morgan.'

Dawlish thought quickly. If this man knew anything about the attack on Georgette, it was extremely unlikely that he would have come here. Once he had reached the mews he would have guessed his, Dawlish's, identity and taken himself off, possibly sending a warning to Morgan that he was being sought.

'Do we know a Mr. Morgan?' asked Tim.

'I was asked to give him a message,' said Dawlish chidingly. 'Don't you remember?'

'I don't know where Mr. Morgan is just now but I can hand on the message the first time I see him,' promised Smith. He looked smugly pleased with himself, and glanced towards the door, as if now eager to go. 'Mr. Morgan often comes to the *Go-Getter*,' he went on, 'and he might look in tomorrow.'

'Nice of you,' said Dawlish. 'Tell him the message is through Georgie—Mr. Brown—will you?'

'Brown?'

'Brown.'

'I'll be delighted.'

'You're very good,' said Dawlish. 'Lot of trouble for you, I'm afraid.'

Smith hid a smile, obviously thinking that Dawlish did not realize what he had given away. As he moved to the door Dawlish made a sign to Tim: *hold him.*

Tim nodded.

In the hall he began chatting garrulously. Dawlish switched off the light, and climbed quickly out of the window. Letting himself hang at full length, he was just able to touch the ground.

He was hiding in a shadowed doorway when at last Tim allowed Smith to leave.

The man from the *Go-Getter* obviously had no idea that he might be trailed, and walked briskly towards Piccadilly. Dawlish followed on the other side of the road. They passed a policeman who was also keeping a special watch on the flat, and was doubtless puzzled by Dawlish's actions. When they reached the main road, Smith looked about him, obviously for a taxi.

Dawlish allowed Smith to get well ahead of him, then hailed a taxi himself.

'Where to?'

'I'll tell you in a minute,' Dawlish said.

He pushed a pound note through the front window, and told the driver to pull into the kerb.

Presently Smith, successful at last in securing a cab, bowled past.

Dawlish tapped on the window.

'Follow it, will you?'

The driver grunted, and started off again as the other taxi passed. They drove down Haymarket to Trafalgar Square and along the Strand and Fleet Street. So they were heading for the East End, Dawlish mused. Both cabs were easily in sight of one another, but two private cars were also in the little stream of vehicles and so far there was no need to fear that Smith would suspect that he was being followed.

At Aldgate, the other cars turned off the main road.

Dawlish leaned forward.

'Drive past him,' he said, 'but don't go too far ahead.'

Dawlish sat back, knowing they were in the Mile End Road, wondering where he had heard the name of the street recently mentioned. Bert had said he would always be found at Joe Speller's, in the Mile End Road.

He leaned forward quickly.

'Do you know a doss-house run by Joe Speller?' he asked.

The cabby gave a laconic nod of assent.

'Go past it, but let me know which it is.'

The driver turned his head as they passed a public house on the left hand side of the road, and jerked his thumb towards the right. Dawlish saw a dim light over a sign bearing the words: *Cheap Beds*. His cabby slowed down.

Smith's taxi pulled up outside the doss-house.

'Take the first turning and stop,' ordered Dawlish.

The taxi swung off the main road and pulled up with a jerk. Dawlish leapt out.

'Wait, please,' he called over his shoulder, and hurried towards the Mile End Road.

Smith was standing outside the open door of the doss-house. Dawlish crossed the road, walking slowly with a slightly uneven gait, as if he were not quite sober. He drew within two shops of the doss-house and dodged into a doorway.

'I tell you he ain't here!' exclaimed a man in a harsh voice. 'It's no use thinking—'

'But I know he is!' insisted Smith. 'And I must see him urgently. Tell him that Mr. Marino of the *Go-Getter* is here.'

CHAPTER NINETEEN

LEN MORGAN

Dawlish heard the first speaker mutter in annoyance, but 'Smith's' persistence was having its effect.

'Wait here,' the man growled, and a moment later the door of the doss-house closed and 'Smith'—alias Marino—was left standing on the doorstep.

The wait seemed unending.

Marino, too, seemed to think so. As he lit a cigarette Dawlish saw his scowl of impatience.

The door opened again.

This time a much shorter man appeared.

'Let's 'ave a look at 'im, Morgy,' a man said.

Dawlish drew in his breath; that was Bert May's voice!

After a quick inspection he drew Marino into the house. Dawlish stepped from his hiding-place, and gently tried the door.

It was locked.

He waited, hearing a murmur of voices inside. He would have given much to be able to hear what was being said.

The voices suddenly became louder.

'Sure, Paul, I'm grateful. I won't forget it.'

'That's fine, Len, that's fine!'

The door opened.

Dawlish pulled out his gun and stepped forward. Marino, Len Morgan and Bert May were standing in front of him, staring in astonishment.

The silence could be felt.

'Good evening,' murmured Dawlish. 'Keep quite still, all of you.'

Taken completely by surprise, the three men obeyed, the man who must be Len Morgan a little in front of the other two.

'Now look—' began Bert.

'I'll do the looking,' Dawlish said. 'Marino, I want to talk to you.'

He took a step forward, his eyes on the *Go-Getter*'s manager, but at the last moment he swung round and grabbed Morgan's arm. Morgan was off his guard and Dawlish jerked him out on to the pavement, his gun still covering the other two.

Three men loomed up from the murky shadow of the hall; hefty-looking fellows prepared for trouble.

'Shut that door, Bert!' snapped Dawlish.

Bert kicked the door to with his foot. The tramp could only delay matters inside for a moment, and time was all too short. Dawlish swung Morgan round and pressed the gun into the small of his back.

'Run,' snapped Dawlish, and the man, now in a state of abject terror, started away with Dawlish at his heels. A moment later the doss-house door opened and there were sounds of shouts and pursuing footsteps. He urged Morgan on and they rounded the corner where Dawlish's taxi was waiting. He reached the cab, wrenched the door open, and pushed Morgan in on to the floor.

'They're going to beat us up. Off as quick as you can,' he shouted to the taxi-man.

The cab moved forward as three men turned the corner. It

gathered speed and after a turn or two they were back in the Mile End Road, going at a good pace.

The driver half-turned his head.

'Where to now?'

'Alyth Mews,' said Dawlish, 'and in case I forget, tuck these away.'

He handed five pound notes to the driver, then turned back to Morgan, who, breathing heavily, seemed dazed by the speed of events.

Dawlish offered him cigarettes. After a moment's pause, Morgan took one. Dawlish flicked on his lighter.

'Know me?'

'You're—you're Dawlish. What do you want?'

'A little heart-to-heart talk with you,' said Dawlish.

Morgan said in a hoarse voice: 'How much will you take to let me go?'

Dawlish hesitated, looking at the man, whose face was visible in the street lamps one moment and lost in the shadows the next. Morgan was serious—and frightened. He was nothing like the strong man Dawlish had expected to find.

'Five hundred?' muttered Morgan.

'We'll see,' said Dawlish.

There was no reason why the man should not remain hopeful; if he thought that a bribe might work, he would be inclined to talk more freely.

They sat back until the cab reached Alyth Mews. The lamps shone on a policeman who looked at them curiously. Morgan's body tensed when he saw the uniform, but Dawlish wished the constable a cheerful good night, thanked the cabby, and led the way up the steps. He was not surprised when the door opened and Tim peered out.

'All safe,' he called. 'And we've another guest.'

In the bright light of the front room, Dawlish studied Morgan's face. He looked as if he hadn't washed for several days, and his clothes were old and worn—certainly not the clothes to be expected of a friend of Georgette's.

'I'll make it a thousand in cash,' Morgan said eagerly.

'Not so fast, Morgan. Business first. I mean to get the information I want. Don't make any mistake about that.'

'I don't know what you want,' protested Morgan. 'I—I was framed for a job, that's why I went into hiding.'

'Not quite so brave now as you were with Georgette, are you?' asked Dawlish.

A glint appeared in Morgan's eyes.

'Did she—'

Dawlish said: 'She hasn't told the police and I haven't seen them yet, but if we have any trouble from you, I'll call them. Yes, the flat's being watched, you needn't hope that your friends will be able to rescue you,' went on Dawlish.

'Now listen to me. I know that you attacked Fairweather and framed Georgette. I know you planned to murder Georgette, making it look like suicide, and that when she was arrested you went to earth. I know you encouraged Georgette to make up to the old man, and when it was obvious that the trick wasn't going to work, you used violence. What I *don't* know is—why?'

Morgan licked his lips.

'I—I was told—'

'And I'm not going to believe that you received orders and knew nothing about reasons behind them,' said Dawlish. 'If you try that game, you'll be in Cannon Row before you can turn round.'

Morgan said: 'I had to do it!'

'Who made you, and why?' demanded Dawlish.

'I don't know who. I had messages from a runner, but I don't know who they came from,' cried Morgan. 'It's no use thinking I do, I just don't know!'

There was a long silence—a frightening quiet. Morgan looked from one to the other, his eyes darting to and fro. At last, Dawlish nodded.

'How shall we start?' asked Tim.

'The usual way,' said Dawlish.

'Start what?' gasped Morgan.

Dawlish said grimly: 'I'm going to make you talk, Morgan, and the quicker you begin the better it will be for you.' He leaned forward. 'Well?' he said.

'I'll tell you what I know,' cried Morgan, trembling violently. 'I'll tell you!'

Dawlish said: 'Get him a drink, Tim.'

Tim poured out a weak whisky-and-soda. Morgan drank it down eagerly. Dawlish watched him with a feeling of great disappointment. There was no strength in this man; at first it had seemed possible that he was the leader of the organization; now Dawlish felt quite sure that he was not.

Did he know enough to help?

Morgan said: 'I—needed that. Dawlish, I'll tell you everything I can, but—'

He broke off, for footsteps sounded on the steps. He turned towards the window, and there was terror in his eyes.

'That's the police!' he gasped. 'You've got to hide me, you've got to hide me!'

The front door bell rang.

CHAPTER TWENTY .

MORGAN'S STORY

'Watch him, Tim,' said Dawlish.

Tim nodded and Dawlish went into the hall. He ignored the trembling Morgan, although he was astonished at the state of the man's nerves. The bell rang again.

He opened the front door, and was almost knocked down by Richard Lloyd's tempestuous entrance.

'I expected you to come round a long time ago,' Lloyd cried in a harsh voice. 'I couldn't get to sleep and—'

Dawlish closed the door and smiled at the younger man, whose face was lined with anxiety.

'Didn't the police tell you I was back?'

'I heard you were free,' said Dawlish.

'Then why—'

'There have been other things to do,' Dawlish told him. 'If you'd keep calmer, you know, you'd get on much better. I've a friend of yours in here.'

'A—friend?'

'Well, a friend of Georgette's,' said Dawlish.

He opened the door and ushered Lloyd into the room.

He could not see Lloyd's face, but watched Morgan's closely; it showed recognition and astonishment. He half-rose from his chair.

Lloyd said: 'What's he doing here?'

'Paying a social visit,' said Dawlish.

'He looks as if he's been hiding in a cellar,' said Lloyd, contemptuously. 'I—Dawlish!'

'Well?'

'Does *he* know anything about this affair?'

'I think he might,' said Dawlish, 'and he's offered me a thousand pounds to let him go free. He *is* a friend of Georgette's, isn't he?'

'He's just a hanger-on,' sneered Lloyd. He crossed the room, without taking his gaze off Morgan. 'How much does heknow?'

'We're just going to find out,' said Dawlish blandly. 'Don't worry if we have to get rough with him, he may need a little coaxing now and again.' He turned to Morgan. 'Now we'll have your story.'

Morgan reiterated that he had received his instructions through Bert May or through other messengers who sported pieces of red ribbon in their buttonholes. He maintained that he did not know from whom the orders came. As the story came out, confirming everything Georgette had told Dawlish—except that Morgan did not say that she was married—Lloyd stood watching him with feverishly bright eyes. Lloyd looked as if he would gladly murder the man, and Morgan was undoubtedly more afraid of Lloyd than of Dawlish or Tim.

He admitted attacking Fairweather.

He admitted attempting to frame Georgette and changing the tablets, so that her death would be taken for suicide.

He maintained that he had not planned any of these things, but had been forced to carry them out.

He also admitted a dozen crimes—blackmail, dope-trafficking, confidence tricks, gaming, smuggling—none of them as a big operator, he swore, but enough to send him down for ten years if the police learned about them. Now that he had begun to talk, he wanted to make a clean breast of the whole story.

When he had finished, Lloyd rasped:

'I'd like to wring his neck!'

'It isn't a hanging job yet,' Dawlish said, 'and the police can take care of him.'

'Dawlish!' Morgan jumped up. 'You promised me—'

'That I would think about a bribe,' said Dawlish, 'and I've done all the thinking I'm going to. In any case you'll be safer in Cannon Row, Morgan. Your boss isn't going to let you roam about.'

'You—you swine!' gasped Morgan. 'You promised me I'd be all right!' He was so frightened that he was on the point of tears, and Lloyd looked at him contemptuously.

Dawlish telephoned Scotland Yard. Munk answered him.

There was much activity during the early hours of the morning. Among other things, Divisional and Yard police raided the doss-house, and took Speller into custody.

Marino was picked up at Euston, waiting for a north-bound train.

Bert May could not be found.

Trivett entered his office just before nine o'clock next morning. Munk was already sitting at his desk reading a closely-written document.

'Heard from Dawlish?' he demanded.

'Not since last night,' said Trivett. 'Has he been in?'

'He hasn't been *in,* but he's made us a present,' said Munk. 'I don't know why it is we search for a man for a week and can't lay our hands on him, and Dawlish digs him up in a few hours. He's got Len Morgan.'

Trivett exclaimed: 'Dawlish *found* him?'

'That's right—and got a statement which I made Morgan repeat. It's on your desk, duly signed, and a further report from Dawlish.'

Trivett skimmed through the statement, then read it more carefully. Everything which Morgan had told Dawlish was written there. He then picked up the report which Dawlish had written before he had gone to bed. When Trivett had finished, the two men looked at each other, frowning.

'We've got to find out what's behind it,' Munk said. 'All we've got so far is that tall story that Dawlish told us about this Max, whoever he is. Dawlish says he's done a bunk—you read that, I suppose. And then there's the cove who was murdered at Staines—we haven't identified him yet.'

'We will,' said Trivett.

'If you ask me, Dawlish knows a lot more than he's told you,' said Munk. 'Still, I suppose we ought to be grateful. Going to put Morgan up before the beak this morning?'

'Yes,' said Trivett.

'Then you'll have to hurry,' said Munk, 'there's a pretty full list.'

Morgan was remanded in custody for eight days. No one in the public gallery appeared to take the slightest interest in the case.

Dawlish woke up a little after ten o'clock, and after a cup of tea, a quick bath and a shave, was ready to meet Tim over a late breakfast. During the meal Dawlish was quiet and Tim, who knew him perhaps better than any other man, kept up a series of absurd remarks, occasionally bringing a fleeting smile to Dawlish's face.

At last, Dawlish said: 'No, Tim, I'm a long way from satisfied. What do you make of it?'

'A nice puzzle,' said Tim, judicially, 'but not beyond solution. It was a bit of a shock to find Morgan one of the rearguard and not the villain of the piece, wasn't it?'

'It was,' agreed Dawlish. 'And if he works for someone else—'

'Who?'

'I'm much more interested in why,' said Dawlish. 'All preconceived notions seem to go by the board now. The armaments talk—you know, the more I think about it, the more likely it seems to me that Maxie put one across me.' Dawlish rubbed his chin and went on ruefully: 'Certainly Bert May did.'

'Ah,' said Tim, 'I wondered when you were going to get round to that.'

'I don't know what to think about him,' Dawlish admitted. 'The marriage business seems so fantastic. Georgette may not have had much social polish when she was young, but she was always a beauty. Why did she marry a man like Bert May?'

'Young love,' sighed Tim. 'Or more likely, money. He may have been rich, and lost the lot. Any chance of finding him?'

The front door bell rang.

'Our little Richard again, I fancy,' said Tim, looking glum. 'Why not tell him that his beloved is a married woman? He will probably be so shocked that we shan't have any more trouble with him. While he thinks there's half a chance to marry Georgette, he'll continue to be a pain in the neck.'

Tim moved languidly to the front door and opened it, Dawlish behind him.

'Good morning,' greeted Bert May.

* * *

After a startled pause, Dawlish drew the little man into the hall.

'Tim, meet Mr. Herbert May,' said Dawlish.

Tim gulped.

'Er—have a drink, Mr. May?'

'Now that's what I call the right idea,' said Bert, as Tim led the way into the sitting-room and poured out a tankard of beer. 'Here's to your good luck—and to my wife!' He drank, wiped his mouth with the back of his hand, and grinned up. 'Has she told you?'

'Yes, she told me,' said Dawlish. 'What made you come? The police are still watching the flat, you know.'

Bert shrugged his shoulder.

'It's two to one they won't recognize me,' he said confidently. 'The fact is—' his expression was both cunning and disarming— 'I found out who you are, and I thought you'd put in a good word for me. I'm tired of being hunted from pillar to post, and thought I might settle down for a change.'

He drank with relish, looking at Dawlish speculatively over the rim of his tankard.

'Have another,' offered Tim.

'Certainly—since you ask me.'

Dawlish's smile broadened.

'Bert, I'm glad to know you,' he remarked, feelingly, 'such a prodigious thirst is worth studying!'

Bert lifted the replenished tankard with a grin.

'Sure that's all you want?'

'Well, not entirely. You haven't told me everything, have you?'

'Not by a long way,' admitted Bert cheerfully. 'But what I did tell you was true enough.'

'Len Morgan employed you, didn't he?'

Bert nodded.

'As well as the others wearing the red ribbon?'

'I wouldn't go so far as to say that,' said Bert, cautiously. 'My job was to watch Georgie.'

'Ah,' said Dawlish.

'Now don't get me wrong,' said Bert. 'I've got nothing against Georgie. She married me for my money certainly, but everybody marries for something however much you disguise it. Money, freedom, legs, what's the difference? The trouble between Georgie and me started when she went on the stage. She won a beauty competition, and I lost the dough,' he informed them glibly. 'So we agreed to part company. Many's the time I thought Georgie'd be after me for a divorce.' He gave another sly grin. 'I wasn't half going to ask for damages! But she never did and so we just left it like that.'

'I see,' said Dawlish, gravely.

'I've picked up a bit of cash where I could, and often it's come from Len Morgan,' said Bert. 'I'm told he was up before the beak for the Fairweather job this morning—serve him right, if he tried to frame Georgie! But you can take this from me—Len never had the guts to do a thing like that for himself. Depend upon it, someone else was with him that night.'

'Yes, there was someone else,' admitted Dawlish.

'Well, what do you want to know?' asked Bert.

Dawlish said: 'These people who called on your wife—have you told me about all of them yet?'

'There's just one other,' said Bert.

'Who's that?'

'The chap I was trying to find the other day, when you met me at Hammersmith,' said Bert. 'Funny thing,' he went on, glancing up with a cunning look in his eyes, 'the minute I saw you, I said to myself—I'll bet he's going to meet the chap I'm after, and I didn't look very hard after that.'

'Thanks very much,' said Dawlish.

'Oh, it's a pleasure,' Bert assured him. 'There's one thing I could have told you at Hammersmith, but it slipped my memory. The beanpole chap had seen someone else that morning—I followed him, so I know.'

'Who was it?' asked Dawlish.

'I've an idea it will interest you very much,' said Bert, 'and it ought to be worth a fiver at least.' He paused, hopefully. 'Or a couple of quid, anyway.'

'Try me and see,' suggested Dawlish.

'Okay. I know you're not mean, whatever else you are. The chap met Flossie. The girl from Woking,' he went on, for Dawlish looked blank, as if this disclosure had made no impression at all.

CHAPTER TWENTY-ONE

DAWLISH PLANS

'So Maxie knows Flossie,' Dawlish observed at last.

'Maxie?' Bert queried.

'Your beanpole,' said Dawlish. 'Bert, I'm very pleased with you.'

'I thought you would be,' said Bert, smugly. 'And I don't mind telling you I wouldn't have told the police about that. Let them find out for themselves, I say.'

'There's one other thing, Bert,' Dawlish said. 'You knew Morgan was hiding at Joe Speller's, didn't you?'

'Of course I did.'

'And who else came to see him at Joe's?'

'No one,' answered Bert earnestly. 'He was so scared I had to go and see who it was before Len would come out of the backroom!'

'Anything else?'

'No, that's the lot—except one thing.'

'Go on.'

'I don't know what will happen to me if anyone knows what I've told you,' went on Bert, now looking really concerned.

'Whoever's paid Len is a nasty bit of work, and my life wouldn't be worth tuppence if it got around. I was wondering if you knew of a nice quiet place where I could stay for a bit—just until it's all over,' he added anxiously.

'You can stay here,' said Dawlish, easily. 'Now if you'd like another drink I'm sure there are a couple of bottles in the kitchen.'

Tim led the way out of the room and shut the door.

Dawlish picked up the telephone, and rang Trivett. Trivett's voice sounded hurried but affable.

'I haven't much time to spare. What's on your mind now?'

Dawlish said: 'Bill, you remember Maxie's story about the director of *Fairweather*'s who quarrelled with the old man—'

'Yes, I've checked it,' Trivett told him. 'An Arthur Frederick Kemble. He was on the board of one of the subsidiary companies, and there was trouble about assets being transferred to the States—the man told you the truth about that, although whether there was any truth in the armaments story I don't yet know. We had been looking for Kemble for some time,' he added. 'He was the man they murdered at Staines. The description tallies, allowing for the facial alterations due to the plastic surgery, and in any case we got his fingerprints from his office.'

'I see,' said Dawlish. 'Thanks, Bill. If you get any confirmation about the armaments story you'll tell me, won't you?'

'Frankly, I think it's all my eye,' Trivett told him. 'I've probed into Fairweather's affairs as deep as I can. There isn't a whisper against him in the City. We know now he didn't lie about the attack in order to save Georgette,' Trivett added, with a chuckle in his voice. 'Morgan's confirmed his story, and—'

'I should be very careful with Morgan if I were you,' said Dawlish.

After a pause, Trivett said: 'I don't like the note in your voice, Pat. What have you got?'

'The whole story, I think,' said Dawlish, 'but I wouldn't yet like to swear that I have. You haven't taken any men off the flat—or from any of the other places that are being watched, have you?'

'No,' said Trivett. 'You needn't be afraid that any precautions will be overlooked. But don't go shooting off on your own again.'

'Only in dire emergency,' Dawlish assured him.

Throughout this conversation Tim, who had slipped back into the room, had been watching his friend intently. Just as Trivett had noticed the inflection in his voice, so Tim saw the change in his expression. There was a hardness there which boded ill for someone—and at the same time a hint of repressed excitement.

Tim knew the signs well.

Dawlish had cut through the inessentials and had caught a glimpse of the solution. Now Tim waited, with his hands in his pockets, a faint smile on his lips.

Dawlish replaced the receiver slowly.

'So you've got the whole story,' Tim murmured.

Dawlish looked at him dreamily.

'I think so. What a fool I was to let Maxie go!'

He told Tim what Trivett had said about Kemble, in quick, graphic phrases.

Tim said: 'And you think Maxie—'

'I think Maxie killed Kemble before he left to pick me up at Hammersmith,' said Dawlish. 'He told me there were two sets of people working against Fairweather—in fact, Tim, there was only one. The impression that there were two was created deliberately, to add confusion and to put me and the police off the scent. Not bad, was it?'

Tim said: 'Not if it's true.'

'Oh, it's true all right,' said Dawlish, confidently. 'Kemble and

Maxie on the one hand, and *Maxie* was the boss, Kemble the stooge, poor chap. And out of the old quarrel with Fairweather, Maxie built up a fine story. Of the armament's racket, for one thing—I don't think there's anything much in that, and Trivett's come round to the same way of thinking. And the suggestion that Kemble was an enemy because of the quarrel he had had, the cleverly suggested motive for his hatred of Fairweather—that Fairweather had framed him over the assets transferred to the United States—wasn't supported by Fairweather himself. I think we'll find that just before the old man was attacked he was told something which suggested this was a vendetta by a personal enemy. Everything was done to conceal the truth—to cover up the true motive.'

'Which was?' asked Tim.

'Unless I'm seeing double, it's what I thought in the first place,' Dawlish said. The dreamy look lingered in his eyes and yet it did not altogether disperse the hint of suppressed excitement. 'Murder of Pop for his money. First step—to get him married to Georgette. If that had come off, then during Pop's lifetime she would have plenty of money—the old boy was generous to her—and also she would have been able to fleece him pretty badly under pressure, of course. So the first attempt was to get at his bank balance through Georgette. Morgan was the intermediary—I think we shall find that Maxie employed him.'

Tim said: 'And Maxie would get the rake-off?'

Dawlish said: 'Oh, a member of the family is mixed up in it somewhere, I think. Flossie with her sullen looks and her dissatisfaction and her hatred of poor Richard—I wouldn't put it past her. I wouldn't put it past Aunt Phoebe, either. It's pretty obvious that the old man slighted them whenever he got the chance. Over the years his treatment of them may have developed a hatred which exploded into violence as soon as someone prompted them to do battle.'

Tim said sharply: 'You're not seriously suggesting that's the answer?'

'I wouldn't call that more than a guess,' Dawlish said. 'But, believe me, it's a family racket.'

'You thought that from the moment Lloyd was nearly killed in that car smash,' Tim reminded him.

Dawlish looked at him absently.

'Yes, didn't I?' he said. 'Tim, we haven't given enough thought to Flossie, you know. When Bert told me that she called on Georgette I began to see the light. Now—what's to be done?'

'Up to you,' said Tim. 'If you think it is a family racket, then Pop's still in the firing line.'

'He's in that all right,' Dawlish said. 'I'm not sure that the police take it seriously. I think we ought to make sure that someone else watches Pop—'

Tim sighed.

'Okay,' he said, resignedly.

Dawlish chuckled.

'Not you, Tim! We want someone *in* the hospital, because if there's a stab at Pop while he's there it will almost certainly be poison. Bill Farningham's the man, as he's at the London. And you and I will go and see Flossie and her mother,' added Dawlish. 'I think we might take Derek, too. I don't think there'll be any more danger for Georgette now that Morgan's in custody.'

'What about Lloyd?' asked Tim.

'You make arrangements with Bill Farningham and telephone Derek,' said Dawlish. 'I'll get Trivett to warn the Haslemere police to redouble their watch, and I'll see Lloyd myself. I think we can call it the beginning of the end,' he said.

*　*　*

Bill Farningham, that promising young doctor who had lost a leg during one of the Dawlish affairs, assured Tim that there would be no difficulty in arranging for careful watch to be kept on Pop Fairweather.

Trivett, whom Dawlish telephoned again, promised that he would see that the police took extra precautions at Haslemere and at the hospital.

Derek Gillow agreed to be at *The Pines* by four-fifteen.

Bert May remained at Tim's flat, which was still kept under observation by the policemen in the mews. By coming to see Dawlish he had burned his boats, and would be content to hide until the affair was over.

Flossie and her mother, according to the police, had been at home all the morning. There was another report from Woking. Aunt Phoebe had obtained the services of another gardener!

All these things Dawlish knew before he went to see Richard Lloyd.

There was no answer when Dawlish rang the bell of Lloyd's flat.

A plainclothes man on duty had told Dawlish that he had not seen Mr. Lloyd that morning, and no one had called.

'Of course,' the man had said, 'there was the postman and the milkman, but that's all. And both of them came away within a couple of minutes. He's alone all right, sir.'

Dawlish stood outside the front door, fingering the key in his pocket. If he used the key, Lloyd would probably lose his temper. He did not want to quarrel with the young man that morning, and so he knocked and rang several times.

Finally he inserted the key in the lock.

When he closed the door the hall was in darkness, and in the rooms the blinds were drawn. Dawlish heard no sound. But for the assurance from the man outside, he would have feared that this was another ambush. He switched on the light and went first into the living-room. It looked as if it had not been dusted for several days. There was cigarette ash in the fireplace, and a bottle of whisky and an empty glass by the side of an armchair.

Dawlish went into the bedroom.

Light came from gaps at the heavy velvet curtains, but he could see Lloyd lying fully-dressed on the bed. He stood quite still. There was no audible sound of breathing. He felt suddenly afraid that the man was dead.

Dawlish went forward and shook him gently. Lloyd stirred but did not wake up. Dawlish raised his eyelids. The pupils were dilated; there was every indication that Lloyd was in a drugged sleep.

He made the man as comfortable as he could, and went into the other room, to telephone Trivett.

Trivett was out, but Munk promised to send a police-surgeon over immediately. That done, Dawlish looked more thoroughly through the flat.

On the mat were two letters, one with the imprint of a stock-broker, the other addressed to Lloyd in block lettering. Dawlish ripped open the envelope.

Inside was a single sheet of folded paper, and on it was a brief message:

I told you the truth on the 'phone last night. Georgette's married—she's been married for years. You silly fool.

That was all.

Dawlish went back into the bedroom and stood looking down at the youngster's face. All suggestion of strength had faded from it.

There was a ring at the front door bell.

'That'll be the surgeon,' Dawlish murmured aloud, and hurried to open the door. But it was only Tim, who had arranged to meet him here.

He led him into the bedroom, indicating the sleeping man.

'Do you think he drugged himself?'

'After getting that message? It might be. I certainly wouldn't like to be sure.' Dawlish gave a mirthless laugh. 'I wouldn't like to be sure about anything, but it looks to me as if Lloyd's been taking drugs for some time. Ah, this will be the surgeon,' he added as the bell rang.

With the police-surgeon was Trivett.

In the opinion of the police-surgeon, Lloyd had been taking morphine for some weeks. Yes, of course, the drug would account for his outbursts of temper and for his general instability. While at the moment he was not in danger, he had obviously taken, or been given, a much larger dose than was his custom.

'It looks as if they intended to kill Pop and Lloyd all right,' Trivett said. 'Pat, what are you going to do at Woking?'

'Talk to Flossie and her mother,' Dawlish said, 'and I'll let you—or the local police—know immediately there's any evidence against them.'

Trivett said slowly: '*Don't* do too much on your own.'

'I won't,' promised Dawlish. 'But as you're leaving it to me, will you withdraw the police to a discreet distance?'

Trivett hesitated before he said: 'For an hour or two, that's all.'

'That's plenty!' Dawlish said. 'And you'll look after Lloyd?'

'Of course.'

'Thanks,' said Dawlish. 'And now, Bill, a tip. I think Maxie pulled the wool over my eyes very neatly.'

*   *   *

It was half past four when the Bentley drew up outside *The Pines*, Tim's Talbot some few yards behind it. Parked in the meadow by the side of the house was Derek Gillow's Lagonda. A thickset man was working in the garden and he looked at the newcomers with undisguised curiosity.

'Well, now for it,' Tim said. 'What are you really expecting, Pat?'

'Anything,' said Dawlish. 'I think—'

He paused.

From the house there came the unmistakable sound of a woman crying. He hurried forward, forgetting what he was about to say, and Tim followed. Through the French window of the sitting-room he could see Derek Gillow and, beyond Derek, Aunt Phoebe. She was lying on the sofa and crying as if her heart would break.

Derek, hearing the newcomers, glanced up quickly. He motioned to the front door. Dawlish nodded and made his way into the house.

'I think I'll stick around here,' said Tim, hovering in the hall. 'Hysterics never appealed to me.'

Dawlish crossed over to Derek, who muttered:

'Thank the Lord you've come, I can't do anything with her.'

'What's the trouble?'

'Daughter Flossie,' said Derek. 'Apparently she took an hour off and came back and told her mother she'd just got married. They had a flaming row. Flossie marched upstairs and is there in high dudgeon, and—' he waved his hand towards the sobbing woman. 'I don't see that it's got anything to do with us,' he added.

After a long pause, Dawlish said slowly:

'Don't you, old chap? A woman can't be made to give evidence against her husband, you know. I think it has plenty to do with us. I'll have to leave Aunt Phoebe to you, though, I want to see Flossie. Who's the happy bridegroom?'

'They wouldn't tell me,' said Derek. 'Well, good luck!'

CHAPTER TWENTY-TWO

FLOSSIE

Flossie was standing by the window of her bedroom when Dawlish knocked, and entered.

She was dressed in a dark, well-fitting suit, and looked much better groomed and more attractive than she had done at their first meeting.

'What do you want?' she demanded.

'To help,' said Dawlish.

'I don't need your help,' snapped Flossie. 'I'm twenty-seven—old enough surely to marry whom, and when, I like. Anyway, it has nothing whatever to do with you,' she finished sullenly.

Dawlish said suddenly: 'Flossie, you know a great deal about what's been going on, don't you?'

'You're talking nonsense!'

'And you have allowed yourself to marry a man who wanted one thing only—the money you'll inherit when your uncle and cousin die,' Dawlish persisted.

'That's a lie!' she screamed.

'*Is* it?' asked Dawlish quietly.

She took a step towards him, her eyes blazing.

'Get out of here! Get out of the house. I hate the sight of you, I wish I'd never seen you. Get out!'

'Who is he?' asked Dawlish.

'Get—*out*!' She took another step forward.

'Is his name Max?' asked Dawlish.

She flew at him then. Momentarily he was carried back by the attack, but he quickly recovered himself and grabbed *her* wrists.

'So it *is* Maxie.'

'You—'

'How long have you known him?' asked Dawlish.

'I'm married to him, I'm his *wife*! You can't make me talk about my husband! *Now* do you understand?'

Dawlish loosened his grip and Flossie wrenched herself free and went for him again, like a termagant. He fended her off more easily this time, and she gave it up and stood looking at him sullenly.

'That won't help,' he said. 'Flossie, I'm not a policeman. I can do a lot of things that a policeman, under strict rules, cannot. I'm going to find out what you know—whether it can be used in evidence or not.'

'I won't say a word!'

'You married Max, knowing of his attempt to murder your uncle,' said Dawlish. 'You had some reason to believe that Fairweather might cut you out of his will, didn't you?'

She drew in her breath.

'Who told you that?'

She cried: 'He told me himself!'

'That was very silly of Pop, wasn't it?' asked Dawlish. 'He didn't know what a heartless little vixen he had for a niece. He didn't realize that you hated him—and hated his nephew—so much that you would be prepared to sink to any depths to get your own back, did he? But as it happened, he wasn't going to cut you out of his will. He'd provided for you and your mother very well. He told me so,' he added, softly.

She stood quite still.

'He—he told you that?' she breathed.

'Yes,' said Dawlish, 'and I'm quite sure it's true, Flossie.'

'He told me that he didn't think I was a worthy person to handle his money, he—' She broke off, and drew in a deep breath. 'I don't believe you,' she finished harshly.

'But it's true,' Dawlish assured her. 'And there was once something between you and Richard that didn't quite come off. You went sour on them both after that, didn't you? And when Max came along and unfolded his plans, you listened to him. Max, a murderer—'

'*I didn't know!*' she screamed. 'I didn't know what he was going to do, it wasn't until after we were married that I discovered what he'd been doing! But I love him—I don't care what he's been doing! But I love him—I don't care what he's done, I love him!'

'I see,' murmured Dawlish. 'Why did he tell you what he'd been up to?'

'He—he told me that you would probably come down here and ask questions,' she said, 'and—and I guessed the truth. But I shan't tell the police; you needn't think I will.'

Dawlish said: 'We aren't having all the truth, Flossie. Max didn't tell you everything.'

'He did!'

'He wouldn't work like that,' Dawlish reasoned, 'he couldn't have been so sure that you would keep silent—you *can* go into the witness box against him if you want to. You're protecting someone, Flossie, you learned the truth somewhere else.'

'I tell you he told me!'

Dawlish paused. He felt sure that she had told him only half the truth. She was protecting someone—and downstairs, crying uncontrollably, was her mother.

He said: 'Flossie, let's have all the truth. In the long run the police are going to find out, you know. It might be better if I learn about it first, I may be able to help.'

'Help! You've done nothing but make things worse,' she accused him.

'Who are you really protecting? It isn't Max.'

'Of course it's Max!'

Dawlish tried again.

'Flossie, I don't believe that you would marry this man suspecting that he was a murderer, and I don't believe that even if married to him you would behave like this except for a very strong reason. Whom are you protecting?'

Flossie set her lips mulishly.

Dawlish felt he had reached an *impasse*. He gazed at her, turning over in his mind the next move.

There was an urgent tap at the door, and Tim's voice came sharply through to him.

'We've made a find, Pat. You ought to see it.'

Flossie cried: 'What have you found?'

'I'll tell you about that later,' Dawlish said.

He slipped the key out of the lock and as she rushed across the room towards him, he opened and slammed the door, locking her in. She banged on the panels furiously.

Tim said urgently: 'Derek's holding the stuff—you'll find that Aunt Phoebe knew a lot more about this business than we thought.'

'Oh,' said Dawlish, blankly.

'I thought all along that that fit of hysteria had a phoney ring.'

Dawlish entered the drawing-room.

Derek Gillow was standing by the piano. Aunt Phoebe, quiet now, was still lying on the sofa.

'I think we've got the whole story,' Derek said, and shot a glance of acute dislike at the silent woman.

CHAPTER TWENTY-THREE

AUNT PHOEBE

Dawlish took the papers.

'Where did you find them?' he asked.

'They were behind the piano,' Derek told him. 'She must have been crazy to keep them there.'

Dawlish glanced through the bundle quickly.

Anyone leaving such evidence lying about was certainly taking risks! They told the story clearly enough of the campaign against Pop Fairweather. In one envelope was a length of red ribbon, of the kind which Bert and the others had worn. There were notes from Morgan, reporting how he had treated Georgette. There was one letter which said that it now looked as if Fairweather was not going to marry Georgette, and others which made it clear that Georgette would have been expected to get every penny she could out of the old man, and to pass it on to Morgan and others. There was even a brief statement showing that once Georgette had gone through a form of marriage with the old man, she would be blackmailed for having committed bigamy. Another note from Morgan said:

Yes, we can buy May's silence, you needn't worry about that.

As he read them, Derek was looking at Aunt Phoebe, to whom several of the letters were addressed.

'Well, what do you make of it?' demanded Derek.

Dawlish raised his eyebrows.

'If we believe all we see, that isn't hard to answer,' he said. 'I think we'd better have Flossie down here and try to force a family showdown.'

Derek nodded and went out.

Dawlish stood with the papers in his hand, looking down at the still form of Aunt Phoebe. If the police had these papers they could come to only one conclusion—and it seemed to Dawlish that there was only one conclusion to be reached. On the other hand, it had been so easy, so remarkably easy.

He said: 'Mrs. Fairweather.'

She did not move.

'Mrs. Fairweather, it won't do any good lying there,' Dawlish said.

She raised her head a little, and spoke in a muffled voice.

'It doesn't matter, nothing matters now my Flossie's thrown herself away on that—that *beast.*'

'It might matter a great deal to Flossie,' said Dawlish. 'Sit up, Mrs. Fairweather, and try to be sensible.'

Reluctantly, she struggled up. Her face was streaked with tears, her eyes were puffy and red-rimmed. One thing was evident; whatever she had done, had been under orders from someone else. She was brainless and weak. He guessed that someone had been behind her all the time, egging her on, perhaps exerting influence—a form of blackmail—when she protested.

The door opened and Flossie entered.

JOHN CREASEY

'What are you doing to my mother?' she demanded.

'The same as I was trying to do with you,' said Dawlish. 'That is, reason with her. Flossie, you know about these papers, don't you?'

He held them up.

Her face blanched, and she drew in a sharp breath as if unable to believe that this thing had happened.

Dawlish said: 'And you've been protecting her, Flossie.'

'She married him because of me!' cried Aunt Phoebe. 'Oh, I would rather have died!'

Flossie walked slowly to a chair and sat down, her expression one of hopeless dejection.

'I'd kill him if he were here. I'd kill him!' cried Aunt Phoebe.

Dawlish said: 'No doubt he'll die in good time, Mrs. Fairweather, and without your assistance. Now, which of you is going to tell me what really happened?'

After a long pause, Flossie began to talk . . .

A few months before, Pop Fairweather had been stung into telling them that they were a worthless, useless couple, and as such could not expect to benefit from his will.

For some time they had brooded over Fairweather's insults and their loss, hating him but accepting his word as final.

One day, Max had come to see them. He had told them much the same story that he had told Dawlish. He said that he had come to invite their help. He had left them seething with anger against Fairweather, and with an excuse for their hatred which was not entirely selfish.

He had come often, after that, paying Flossie much attention—which she had ignored—and eventually discovering that he would get most help from Aunt Phoebe, who was thinking less of herself than of her daughter's future.

162

The first actual crime had been committed six months before, when Aunt Phoebe had gone to London, ostensibly to visit her brother-in-law, actually to steal some papers from his private office. She had been left alone for a while, succeeded in getting the papers, and handed them over to Max, who was waiting for her outside. What was in the papers Aunt Phoebe didn't know, and Flossie had not been told of the incident for some time.

It transpired that as Mrs. Fairweather and her daughter had little income of their own, Fairweather made them a small but adequate allowance, which was the basis of their livelihood. Max now threatened to disclose what she had done—and Aunt Phoebe had known that if Fairweather discovered it, the allowance would cease forthwith. Max also said that he knew Fairweather had not yet altered his will. So she had done what-ever she had been told, sometimes under protest, sometimes overcome by a flood of childish hatred against Fairweather.

She said now that she had not known of, or been told about, everything that was happening. She had known about the plan to make Georgette marry Fairweather, but not about the attack on him. She had known of Morgan, but never seen him. She had allowed a succession of gardeners to visit the house, usually men who wanted to get in touch with Max.

He called at the house after dark and interviewed the men then. What passed between them, said Aunt Phoebe, she did not know.

Then—two days ago—Flossie had discovered the papers, challenged her mother and forced the story out of her. Flossie had been beside herself, and Max had come that evening, laughing at them, showing that nothing could save Aunt Phoebe if the truth were ever learned.

He had not been satisfied with their frightened assurances that they would keep quiet. He had told Flossie that if she married him she need have nothing to fear. If Flossie had realized that he was really planning to get his hands on the Fairweather money, she had, nevertheless, agreed to marry him.

At last, Flossie ended: 'And there just isn't anything we can do, if Max is caught everything will come out.' She looked bleakly at her mother. 'If I'd only known three months ago we might have done something, but now—' She broke off.

Aunt Phoebe said in a flat voice: 'I'll have to go through with it, dear, it can't be helped now. Major Dawlish will have to tell the police, and then Max will be arrested. *You'll* be all right, they wouldn't let that marriage stand—would they, Major Dawlish?'

'Not for a minute,' Dawlish said.

'You can't give yourself up!' protested Flossie, and swung round on him. 'I won't allow that to happen! Mother must go away somewhere, she needn't be caught!'

'But look at the worry it would mean, dear,' said Aunt Phoebe. 'We'd never be able to call our lives our own. I'm sure Major Dawlish will agree with me that it's the only thing to do.'

Dawlish said: 'I think the first thing to do is to find Max. Do you know where he is, Flossie?'

'No,' said Flossie. 'He's never told me where I could find him.' She closed her eyes wearily. 'Oh, what a mess it is!' she cried. 'Don't you see, no one would ever believe mother was *forced* into it, they'd think it was just because she wanted to get her hands on the money.'

Aunt Phoebe stood up.

She looked forlorn and weary, but there was a glint in her eyes of which Pop might have been proud.

'It isn't any use talking any more, I've got to go through with it, and the sooner the better. There are policemen watching the house, Major Dawlish, aren't there? Bring one of them in and tell him. No, Flossie, I'm not going to change my mind, this is the end of it—I can't stand the strain any longer.'

Flossie dropped into a chair.

Dawlish said: 'The police have been withdrawn, Mrs. Fairweather. I was able to arrange that. You know. I'm not sure that we've got all the truth yet.'

Flossie snapped: 'Of course you have. I—oh, what's that?'

The telephone rang through the house.

Tim stepped into the hall, watched tensely by the others, and lifted the telephone.

'This is Mrs. Fairweather's—'

'*Drop that!*' called a man from the front door.

There was a shot and Tim reeled away from the telephone. Derek reached the door as two men rushed in, and one sent him staggering back with a kick that caught him on the shin.

Only Dawlish stood quite still.

Into Flossie's eyes there sprang a gleam which might be of triumph; it was gone in a flash.

Max, gun in hand, sauntered into the room.

About the time that Dawlish reached *The Pines,* the man Wilmot walked along the passages of the Riverside Hospital. He was clad in a white coat with an orderly's armlet, and carried two glasses.

Wilmot reached Pop's private ward.

A uniformed policeman on duty nodded to him.

'I'm to get some dirty glasses out of here,' said Wilmot. 'They couldn't spare a nurse.'

'Don't be long,' warned the policeman.

'Okay.'

Wilmot went in, closing the door behind him.

Pop was sitting up against his pillows. He turned his head with little show of interest.

'I've just come to collect the empty glasses, sir,' said Wilmot.

He approached the bed and, with his back to the old man, put down the fresh glasses and picked up two that were already there. A white tablet slipped from his fingers into a water jug. 'Goodnight, sir.'

''Night!' mumbled Fairweather.

Wilmot moved to the door.

It opened as he touched the handle. Dr. Bill Farningham and the policeman stood in the doorway. Their grim and purposeful position could have but one meaning. Wilmot snatched a gun from the pocket of his coat, while Farningham swung out his right arm. The roar of a shot echoed through the building as Wilmot staggered under the blow. Before he could recover his balance Farningham and the policeman had overpowered him.

As soon as Trivett was informed, he put in a call to Dawlish at Woking.

Aunt Phoebe was so frightened that she could only stand staring, shivering from head to foot.

Dawlish called out: 'How are you, Tim?'

'Forearm—flesh wound,' Tim called, in a matter of fact voice. 'Sorry, old boy.'

'Take it easy,' said Dawlish, looking at Max.

'Now that is very sound advice,' agreed Max, smiling amiably. He looked as likeable and cheerful as when Dawlish had first seen him. 'Hallo, honey,' he added, and touched Flossie's arm.

'Don't touch her!' screamed Mrs. Fairweather.

Max shrugged good-humouredly.

'Who thought of sending the police away, Dawlish?'

'I did,' answered Dawlish.

'You're much too cocky,' said Max.

Dawlish smiled.

'Am I? Wasn't it the only way of making sure that you'd turn up when you knew that I'd come to interview the ladies after the police had gone?'

'Maybe,' said Max, 'but what good has it done you?'

'I've an old-fashioned urge to find out the truth,' said Dawlish.

'An admirable quality—but, alas, doomed to be short-lived. For you're going to be snuffed out, Dawlish—all three of you— just like candles. My dear mother-in-law is going to kill you all and then commit suicide, my poor dear wife will be the only one of the family left alive. And just about now, Wilmot is killing Fairweather,' he continued. 'Lloyd is a drug-addict, I can handle him anyway I like. Got the general idea?'

His tone was light, almost flippant, yet there was an undertone of hardness and Dawlish saw that he was deadly serious. Here, it seemed, was the final working-out of a carefully laid and long-planned crime.

Dawlish spoke into the tense silence.

'And how do you propose to snuff us out?' he asked.

'By shooting you,' Max said, promptly, 'and then the old girl can turn the gun on herself. Flossie will testify that her mother fired every shot, and I'll see that her prints are on the gun.'

'Oh, I've no doubt about that,' said Dawlish. 'It was Flossie who planted those papers behind the piano, wasn't it? To make sure that they would be easily found and that her mother would be blamed. Only she did it a little too soon, and I found the papers before her mother was killed—had it worked according to plan, Mrs. Fairweather would have "committed suicide" and the police would have found this evidence against her. You're not once mentioned in those papers, Max are you? You had a good testimonial from me—'

Max grinned.

'Sure, I worked hard for it! But thanks, Dawlish.'

Dawlish said: 'To get it, you let me leave the Walton house, just to confuse me. And your pretty trick with Wilmot was smart—that was all pretence, to make me think there were two parties after Pop.'

'That's right,' Max agreed, 'but you ought to have thought of it sooner.'

'And you put that show on at the farmhouse, too,' went on Dawlish. 'I think you killed Kemble before you left to meet me. He was getting too difficult, he didn't like so much violence.'

'Well, what an idea!' Max sneered.

'I think you were the boss and Kemble the stooge,' Dawlish went on in the same level voice. 'That's why I thought I'd give you a chance to turn up here, Maxie—I was so anxious to know the truth.'

'It'll do you a lot of good,' Max said scoffingly. 'Supposing you tell me some more?'

One of the gunmen said uneasily: 'We don't want to stay too long, Maxie.'

'We're all right,' Max said. 'We saw the police move off, didn't we? Go on, Dawlish—tell me what you *think* you know.'

Dawlish said: 'Right! Here it is, then. Your talk of an armaments racket was all boloney. Kemble did try to swindle Fairweather and transfer assets abroad, and you used him to get at the old man. This is a family affair. Fairweather is to be murdered so that his surviving relatives inherit his fortune and you collect the proceeds. Maybe Lloyd's taken to drugs, as you say. But dear Flossie—'

'What are you saying?' moaned Mrs. Fairweather.

Dawlish sent a glance of compassion towards the woman.

'Flossie's responsible for part of this,' he said. 'She plotted and planned, and Max helped her. Eh, Flossie?'

The girl moistened her lips.

'Flossie, it isn't true!' whimpered Mrs. Fairweather.

'Oh, it's true enough,' said Flossie, with a new, hard note in her voice. 'Max showed me the way out—'

Her mother dropped onto the couch, burying her face in her hands.

Dawlish felt quite sure that Max's men were watching the house from all sides. Deliberately he, Dawlish, had walked into the trap. He had learned most of the truth but there *must* be a way out. If the police had gone too far—

Max was on the crest of a wave.

'So we're getting near the truth,' Dawlish said. 'First of all you thought you'd work through Georgette. If you had made Fairweather marry her, you'd have fleeced him through her—holding the threat of disclosure that she'd committed bigamy over her head all the time. When that didn't work, you turned to violence. You wanted results too quickly, Max, that was your mistake.'

'It isn't I who've made the mistakes,' said Max and laughed. 'You haven't found it all out yet, Dawlish.'

'He knows enough,' Flossie said, in a sharp voice, 'and we ought to hurry.'

'There's just one thing you *don't* know,' Dawlish said to her. 'You'd better wait for it.' He looked at the girl contemptuously, then said deliberately: 'Richard Lloyd died from an overdose of morphine poisoning this morning.'

Flossie gasped: 'He died? I—no! That's a lie!' She swung round on Max in a sudden fury of rage. 'Did you do it? Did you—'

'He's lying to you!' cried Max in sudden alarm. 'Don't believe him!'

Dawlish said evenly: 'Max thought he was better out of the way.'

She flung herself at the man and his gun fell to the ground.

Dawlish leapt at Max, flooring him with a single blow. He dodged to one side as the man at the door fired, bellowing:

'At him, Derek!'

Derek Gillow launched himself bodily on the man. There was a shot but it came too late to prevent Derek from reaching his victim, whose gun went flying.

Tim staggered in, pale-faced but with his eyes glowing.

Others were running across the garden now, but before they reached the house Derek and Tim had barricaded the room, piling chairs before the door. Two shots whizzed harmlessly through the panels. Max lay dazed on the floor, while Dawlish watched the window. If they could only hold out for twenty minutes or so, surely the shooting would by then have aroused attention.

Suddenly Flossie rushed at him, her lips curled back. Grappling with her he heard over the din of wails and curses Derek's voice raised in jubilation.

'Take it easy! Take it easy! The police are here!'

The telephone call had been from Trivett—and he had heard the shot over the wires. Within a minute, he had telephoned the Woking police, who had quickly closed in on the house.

Dawlish talked for what seemed a long time.

Flossie, Max and the men who worked for him were under arrest, and Trivett had told Dawlish of the abortive attempt on Fairweather's life. Aunt Phoebe had made her confession in a husky, emotionless voice—she was stunned by what had happened; Dawlish knew that, when the trials came, the law would be merciful with her. Max and Flossie and Wilmot would undoubtedly receive the full sentence for complicity in murder.

All these things were apparent as Dawlish talked and Trivett listened.

Derek Gillow and Tim were at Woking Hospital, both suffering from gunshot wounds but neither of them in a serious condition.

'And so that's that,' Dawlish said, when he had finished. 'Satisfied now, Bill?'

'I suppose I ought to be,' conceded Trivett, 'But one thing puzzles me.'

'What's that?'

'You say you made Flossie break down when you pretended that Lloyd was dead. How does that square up?'

Dawlish chuckled.

'Bill, you've spotted the weakness! Max wasn't the real leader, *Lloyd* was.'

'Flossie and Lloyd have been in this together, the marriage with Max was one of convenience—in fact I doubt whether they *were* married,' Dawlish went on into a tense silence. 'It was Lloyd who was the kingpin of the entire plot, and a superb actor. First the marriage to Georgette was planned; then, seeing his chance, he tried to kill the old man and frame Georgette for the murder.'

Trivett said sharply: 'Can you prove it?'

'He'll still be feeling the effect of the drug,' Dawlish said, 'if you're at him the moment he begins to come round I think you'll get a confession. Anyhow, Maxie will probably talk to save himself. I'd try Maxie first, Bill. And I'll be surprised if you don't learn what you want.'

Max talked freely.

Lloyd was arrested later that evening, so befuddled by the

drug that when confronted by Max's statement, he didn't attempt to deny it.

The story unfolded quickly.

In the beginning, Lloyd had lost a large sum of money, and was in desperate straits. He and Flossie were in love, and each was treated scornfully by Fairweather. Out of their cupidity and hatred of their uncle the plot was conceived. When their plan to compromise Georgette and, after her 'marriage' to Fairweather to blackmail her failed, Lloyd decided to murder his uncle and throw the blame on Georgette.

One trick was built upon another. Lloyd had given his tortuous mind full reign, caring nothing who suffered provided he and Flossie came through safely. And in the end the whole elaborate structure came tumbling down.

Dawlish crossed the floor of the smoking-room at the Carilon Club as Pop Fairweather picked up his unopened *Times*. He put it down again.

'I see you are going to ask me how I am, so I will save your time and mine by saying I am perfectly well. I won't pretend that the trial wasn't a shock to me, but I shall recover. Tell me, how is Georgette?'

'Well, and happy,' said Dawlish.

'I heard that she was seeking a divorce and contemplated marriage with a friend of yours.'

'That's true,' said Dawlish.

'Hmm. I don't know whether to condole with or congratulate your friend,' said Pop. 'I suppose it is for the best.'

Dawlish smiled.

'Hmm, yes. Dawlish, you never told me just *how* you managed to unravel the remarkably complicated affair. That man Trivett tells me that you were chiefly responsible.'

Dawlish smiled.

'Trivett grossly exaggerates. How is Aunt Phoebe?'

'Very well,' said Fairweather. 'She has given up *The Pines* and is coming to keep house for me. You need not worry about her.'

'I wouldn't say that,' said Dawlish. 'I think I ought to commiserate, being housekeeper to you is a full time job.'

Fairweather's wintry eye twinkled.

'I suppose I asked for that. In point of fact I'm commissioned by her to say "thank you", Dawlish. I hope you will also accept my warmest thanks.'

They shook hands.

'Remarkable! Quite remarkable!' Pop murmured; but whether he was referring to Dawlish's grip or his prowess in detecting was not clear.

Opening *The Times* Pop sank, with a bland sigh, into his chair.

ABOUT THE AUTHOR

John Creasey, born in 1908, was a paramount English crime and science fiction writer who used myriad pseudonyms for more than six hundred novels. He founded the UK Crime Writers' Association in 1953. In 1962, his book *Gideon's Fire* received the Edgar Award for Best Novel from the Mystery Writers of America. Many of the characters featured in Creasey's titles became popular, including George Gideon of Scotland Yard, who was the basis for a subsequent television series and film. Creasey died in Salisbury, UK, in 1973.

THE PATRICK DAWLISH MYSTERIES

FROM OPEN ROAD MEDIA

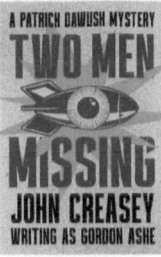

INTEGRATED MEDIA

Find a full list of our authors and titles at www.openroadmedia.com

FOLLOW US
@OpenRoadMedia

www.ingramcontent.com/pod-product-compliance
Lightning Source LLC
Chambersburg PA
CBHW050337110726
47899CB00007B/2535